Total-E-Bound Publishing books by HK Carlton:

Swap

I0617694

LOST TIME

HK CARLTON

Lost Time
ISBN # 978-1-78184-601-8
©Copyright HK Carlton 2013
Cover Art by Posh Gosh ©Copyright January 2013
Interior text design by Claire Siemaszkiewicz
Total-E-Bound Publishing

LOST TIME

Dedication

I would like to dedicate Lost Time to Amy, Stacey, and everyone at Total-E-Bound. Thank you for everything.

To my British, Scottish and Canadian heritage and the kind-hearted people in Wales who stopped to help a stranded tourist, which ultimately inspired this story. And finally to my own hunky Highlander — I await…

Chapter One

Hannah Keys rode sleepily on a bus headed for Wales. She was alone, thanks to her friend Cassidy who'd flaked on her at the last possible moment. Hannah and Cassie had been planning this trip to the UK for years—a month in England, Wales, Scotland and Northern Ireland, a week for each.

Twenty-four years old, Hannah—a Canadian girl raised by her transplanted English mother—used to sit and listen for hours as her mum told stories of growing up in London, of the family she'd left behind, including Hannah's father. His death had been the catalyst that had sent her mum fleeing to different shores before Hannah was born, to get away from the memories that were far too painful. Her mum had talked of friends from school, the beautiful countryside, of haunted castles and the amazing architecture that stood the test of time.

Hannah had read everything she could get her greedy little hands on, whether it be a history book or a historical romance novel or the old books her mum had brought over. Hannah had sat for hours and looked at the old photos, including one of her dad. She'd always been enamoured with anything English — the monarchy, the castles, and the history — while Scotland and Ireland held their own share of legend and lore that lured her imagination. Her mother had made everything sound so romantic, and now that her mum was gone, Hannah wanted and needed to see where her mother had come from.

The plan had always been to see the UK with her mum, but when her mother got sick, everything had changed. But she had made Hannah promise that she would still take the trip. That was when her best friend Cassie had stepped in to take her mother's place. And it hadn't hurt that Cassie had just seen *300*, starring Gerard Butler. After that, Cass was convinced that every other guy in the UK might possibly look like Gerard, and she was all in.

At least Hannah had thought she was all in. But as she'd stood in line at the airport, with images of old stone castles and moors in bloom, rowdy pubs and Stonehenge running through her overly-excited mind, waiting for her BFF to show, the last thing she'd expected was for her cell phone ring and have her FBFF — *former* best friend forever — abandon her. Although Cassie had attempted to apologise enthusiastically, it would be a cold day when Hannah accepted it.

"What do you mean you're not coming?" Hannah had asked through gritted teeth.

"Paul proposed last night!" she'd gushed. "Isn't that the best news ever, Hannah?"

Hannah might have been happy for her at any other time, or if she hadn't thought Paul was a complete dick and had only asked Cassie this life-altering question the night before the big trip because he didn't want Cassie to go off without him…even though it had been planned long before he'd even met her. But, as much as Hannah disliked Paul as a person, she secretly envied what Cassie had with him. She wanted that for herself—someone to share her life with, someone to love and who loved her in return. She hadn't allowed herself to be close to anyone since her mum had passed away. Hannah was determined never to love someone so completely again. It only led to heartache. Besides, she'd never had much luck with guys or relationships, anyway. They only wanted one thing, and it wasn't her heart.

"And you can't meet me *why?*" Hannah asked a little too loudly, causing other waiting passengers to look in her direction.

"Because I don't want to leave him now," she whined, as if that should explain it all.

"But you can spend the rest of your life with good old Paul after we get back. Cassie, we've planned this trip for seven freakin' years, and I'm standing in the airport all by myself waiting for—"

"Oh, I knew you'd understand, Hannah. You're the best. I'll see you when you get back and you can tell me all about the Gerards that you shagged without me. Send me a postcard from Ireland. I'll make this up to you, Hannie, I promise, 'kay? Love you. Bye-bye."

The cell went quiet and Hannah resisted the urge to spike the damn thing on the floor. She spent the next thirty minutes panicking and pacing, trying to convince herself not to go back home.

You've come this far. You're so close. Everything you've dreamt about is only a plane ticket and an ocean away.

She was insane to travel unaccompanied. Not only the danger, but what fun would it be to sightsee and bar-hop? *Single White Female* abroad and alone. She was just asking for trouble. Right?

Damn it, she argued, she'd scrimped and saved and budgeted for so long and she'd already spent the money. Besides, she *really* wanted to go, with or without Cass. This was her dream. And she'd vowed to her mother on her deathbed that she would take this trip.

Despite the last-minute problem, something inside her pulled her in that direction. It always had. Perhaps, if she was honest with herself, she should have realised that Cassie had never been as excited about this journey as she had.

So, for once, she threw caution to the wind and handed her ticket to the agent. "One for London."

Hannah held Cassidy's ticket in her hand. "Can I cash this ticket in?" she inquired, almost as an afterthought. "My friend's not going to be able to make it."

"Sure, but you'll only get about eighty per cent back."

"That's fine." Hannah handed it over to the ticket agent. "It's not my money, anyway," she said, under her breath. But she had every intention of spending it. Cassie owed her that much. *Damages*, Hannah reasoned, *along with mental stress and suffering, not to mention abandonment.*

* * * *

Hannah had boarded the plane headed for Heathrow with raw excitement humming through her. But after a week of sightseeing all by herself, she was second-guessing her decision. Vacations weren't meant to be experienced alone.

She'd seen the Tower of London and Big Ben. One day, she had taken a bus tour of castles, including Windsor—on the next day, she saw cathedrals and abbeys. Another one she had spent shopping, buying touristy trinkets and a T-shirt that read *Kiss Me, I'm Scottish,* which she had every intention of wearing for that leg of the trip.

She had also spent a day on the Internet, trying to locate the house that her mum had grown up in. When she found it, she had called a taxi and told the driver the street address, but when he took her there, the house had been torn down. So Hannah had taken a picture of the street sign and sadly returned to her hotel room.

Another day, she had taken a double-decker bus and visited the London Eye. She had even found the courage to ask another tourist to take her picture standing near it. But she hadn't ridden the enormous wheel. Another thing she would have liked a companion for.

Hannah rested her head against the cool glass and looked out the window of the bus headed for Wales, grateful to be on the next leg of the trip. But, more and more, she was thinking of cutting her losses and just heading home. She'd imagined having such a wild time—sightseeing through the day with Cass, hitting the clubs at night, dancing, maybe even hooking up with some hot guy for just one night before moving on. It wasn't as if she were anti-social, or not good at making friends. She'd just wanted to share this with Cass.

Hannah knew that she could get all dressed up and go to the pubs—she didn't need Cass for that. She was pretty enough and garnered attention all on her own, but it just didn't feel right. When she'd tried, she'd

HK Carlton

had no fun, no dancing—no shagging, as she and Cass had joked. She'd even had a couple of men approach her as she'd sat alone, eating a meal. However, when she'd just given them a cool smile, they'd nodded and gone on their way.

Hannah closed her eyes as a wave of loneliness descended over her, making her feel empty.

Someone tapped her shoulder.

"What?" She must have dozed off, she realised. Hannah sat up groggily, looking at the young guy. She thought he'd spoken to her in Welsh, which she didn't understand. It was such a guttural-sounding language.

"Pardon, I'm sorry, can you speak English?" Hannah asked, hopeful.

He couldn't be more than eighteen, she guessed. He grinned and spoke slowly. "This is the last bus tonight. This is as far as it goes."

"Oh! Oh no! Did I miss my stop?" She had a sinking feeling.

"I don't know. Where were you headed?"

"The girl back in London said Llandeilo, but much more throaty-sounding than that. She said that I could get a ticket there and transfer to another bus to Swansea. That's where I have a room booked."

"You are in Llandeilo." He laughed indulgently at her pronunciation but went along with it.

"Yeah, see? Just like I said, just a little more throaty." Hannah laughed too.

He grinned widely. "You should be able to get a ticket inside to continue on to Swansea. Can I help you with your bags?"

"Oh, you're so sweet. Thank you."

"Are you American?"

"No, Canadian," she answered, turning the little maple leaf pin she had fastened on her windbreaker towards him. She had the same little red symbol tattooed on the inside of her left wrist and a tiny blue one on her right, in homage to her favourite hockey team—the Toronto Maple Leafs.

"Anywhere I might know?" he asked.

"Probably not."

They stepped off the bus and he set the bags at her feet.

"The station is right there." He pointed. "But you'd better hurry—they don't stay open all night. I've gotta go. You'll be all right?" He watched her with concern.

"Yes, thank you. My name's Hannah, by the way," she said, holding her hand out and smiling. "Thanks for your help."

"It's good to meet you, Hannah," he said, taking her hand. "Jakob, they call me Jake." He seemed like a really easygoing, nice kid.

"It was good to meet you, Jake."

"Have a good holiday, Hannah." He waved as he walked off.

Her smile wavered as she picked up her bags. "Yeah. Thanks." She headed into the station.

"Hi," she said, to the woman at the desk. "One for Swansea."

The ticket agent slid a ticket across the counter.

"Thank you," Hannah said, paying then turning away and glancing at the ticket. "Ten?" She checked her watch. It was just past eight p.m. Even this would be bearable if she had someone else to do it with.

She sighed. Two hours? What was she going to do for two hours?

She sat down on one of the padded benches. Her butt had barely touched the seat when the ticket agent said, "We close at eight."

Hannah watched her wide-eyed as the woman hefted one of her bags and started towards the door. She placed the bag on the sidewalk outside then turned the sign hanging on a chain from the door.

"You're closing?" Hannah asked incredulously, while she struggled with her carry-on and the other case.

"What am I going to do? Wait outside?" And, as if things couldn't be any worse, it began to piss rain.

The lady pointed to the pub down the street where some sketchy-looking men milled around out front, in the mounting fog. "Perhaps you could go enjoy a cuppa," she suggested.

"I can't…" Hannah paused when she heard the glass door lock behind her, the lights inside darkening.

"Oh, this *is* a magical trip. It just keeps getting better and better," she complained to herself as the rain took on a steady beat. "I swear you are trying to teach me a lesson, Mum," she mumbled, looking up at the wet sky. "But for the life of me I can't figure out what it is. I just want to go home."

She looked down the street. Maybe she could get a cup of coffee in one of the establishments, she thought, but changed her mind when she realised the shadows down by the pub seemed to be moving in her direction.

"This is just great!" she grumbled, looking down the street in the opposite direction, wondering where she would flee to if those shadows came any closer.

Instead a more immediate problem presented itself, as a car slowed and stopped near the kerb and the window began to roll down.

"I'm not a hooker!" she yelled, a second before she realised it was Jake.

He laughed. "I know you're not. Do you need a lift?"

Now what should she do? Take her chances with the shadows closing in on her or drive off with strangers? She didn't like either of her options.

"My gran says you can't stay here," he said — noting her indecision, Hannah suspected.

"Your gran?" Hannah looked closer into the car but couldn't see through the darkness or the rain.

"Yeah, she says there are no more buses tonight."

"But they sold me a ticket." Hannah pulled it out of her inside jacket pocket. "See, it comes at ten...a.m.," she realised belatedly. She threw her hand up in frustration, rolling her eyes.

Jake jumped out of the car. "Pop the boot, Gran," he said, evidently for Hannah's benefit since he then said something in Welsh. He tossed her luggage inside and opened the back passenger's door.

Hannah still hesitated. "Really, Jake, I can't..."

"Sure you can. You can't stay here. We can't leave you."

She ducked into the backseat. "Thank you so much, Mrs..." she said, to the back of the older woman's head.

"You can just call her Gran, Hannah. You'll never be able to pronounce it, anyway." Jake grinned.

Hannah nodded, uncomfortable with that, but he was probably right.

'Gran' started speaking quickly to Jake in Welsh as she pulled away from the bus station.

"Don't mind her," Jake explained, "Gran doesn't feel comfortable speaking English. She's kind of set in her ways. She wants to know the name of your hotel in

Swansea. Sorry, I hope you don't mind—I kinda told Gran all about you. We'll just take you there."

"Oh, no, I couldn't ask you to do that. It's out of your way and it's such a horrible night to drive." Hannah could barely see out of the windshield through the rain and fog.

"What's the name? When Gran gets something in her head, there's no changing her mind."

"Um, Gorman's, I think."

The older woman nodded.

"Yep, we know it. That's a great place. You'll like it," Jake offered.

It seemed pitch black outside. The darkness was eerie as they drove out of town, the fog getting thicker by the second.

"I really appreciate this, Jake."

"Oh, no trouble. I've heard that Canadians are very kind. Maybe when you get back, you can let your country know that we Welsh are just as nice."

"You can bet that I will."

"Besides, Gran comes out every night to get me off the bus. She's nice enough to meet me and drive me the rest of the way home after my shift, since this is as far as the buses travel. My gran's the best." Hannah could hear the genuine affection in his voice.

"Yes, she is," Hannah agreed, smiling, beginning to feel a lot less creeped out by the whole situation. Accepting a ride in a foreign land from two strangers, when no one knew where she was, was probably not the smartest thing she'd ever done. It certainly wasn't something she would normally do, not even if Cass had been with her. But it was the kid's grandmother, for goodness sake. How much safer could it be?

"So specifically, where are you from?" Jake asked, craning in the seat to look at her. "I'm gonna look it up on Google when I get home."

"Have you heard of Toronto?" At his nod, she added, "I'm from a smaller town near there, like a suburb, called Brampton."

"Naw, never heard of it."

"But I work in Toronto."

"Oh? What do you do?"

"I'm in retail. I work at a store, too—a clothing store. Trying to work my way up. My friend Cassie and I are hoping to open our own shop someday. So I'm trying to learn the trade. From the ground up, I guess you'd say."

"Ah oh," Gran said. Hannah understood that—it was pretty universal.

Hannah looked up to see flashing lights. Gran slowed and came to a stop. An officer approached and ducked his head to the window.

Jake's gran and the officer had one of those fascinatingly guttural conversations as Jake translated.

"There's a tree down blocking the entire road. We need to turn around."

Why was this day so difficult? Could nothing go right? It was as though she wasn't supposed to reach Swansea. She should just go home. How many signs did she need to convince her that this trip had been a bad idea?

"He says it's really bad from here on out. I guess you're not reaching Swansea tonight, Hannah, sorry. He's advising all motorists to stay off the roads if it isn't an emergency."

"Well, this is just great. I'm really sorry about all this. Please tell your gran."

He did and she responded, turning the car around.

"Is there a hotel, an inn—a B&B you could drop me at?"

"We know the perfect place for you," Jake said, smiling.

"Thanks. Again." She leant back and rubbed her temples.

"Are you not feeling well?"

"It's just been a long day." *And an even longer week,* she thought miserably.

He let her be. After about fifteen minutes, the car slowed.

"Well, here we are. You can finally end this long day, if you want."

Hannah sat up as they wended their way up a winding drive. A burst of lightning lit up the sky, illuminating the dwelling. It looked like a castle.

"Where are we?"

"This is our farm," Jake informed her proudly.

"Your farm? It looks like a castle."

Jake and his gran exchanged a look.

Jake snorted. "Well, no one has ever said that before."

"Was there nowhere else you could drop me? I don't want to impose. You've already gone out of your way for me."

"It's no trouble."

The car stopped and Jake jumped out to retrieve her bags. Hannah stepped out, only to be battered once again by the cold wind and rain.

"Follow Gran, Hannah, I've got these."

She followed the older woman up the steps and through a massive wooden door. As soon as Hannah crossed the threshold, a weight descended upon her. Her head started to throb and her heart pounded in her ears—the misery of the day finally catching up with her.

From the inside, it looked like a farmhouse should look. It was open-plan and dimly lit. Hannah could see straight through to the kitchen, where a huge, old wooden table dominated the space.

Gran was talking away but Hannah hadn't a clue as to what she was saying. But she followed her lead and removed her wet coat, which Gran promptly hung on a shiny brass coat rack.

"Thank you."

Gran took her arm and towed her towards the kitchen, pulling out a chair from the table. Hannah sat obediently while Gran filled the kettle. She then directed Jake with Hannah's bags up the stairs.

Hannah had felt much more comfortable when Jake was present—at least she could communicate with him.

Hannah's head throbbed steadily and again she found herself rubbing her temples.

Jake and his grandmother spoke quietly when he returned.

"Let me show you your room. Gran will bring you up some tea shortly when it's ready. Can I get you something for your headache?" he asked as he led her up the stairs.

"No, thanks—I have some aspirin in my luggage."

Jake opened the door at the end of the hall. There was an enormous four-poster bed taking up most of the back wall. The rest of the furniture was solid-looking dark wood.

"Oh, Jake, this is a lovely room."

"Yeah, next to Gran's, this is the nicest."

"Then why don't you have this room?"

"This room? Naw, it gives me the creeps."

"What on earth for?" Hannah asked, looking around. It looked perfectly homey.

He shrugged. "I'll pull the drapes for you, to keep any light out." He did so then turned on the adjoining bathroom light for her. "I've gotta go. I've got homework to do and maybe Gran'll even make me some supper. Hope you sleep well."

"Thank you. You've done so much for me."

"No trouble. I hope your headache goes away," he said, closing the door.

Hannah went straight to her bag and took out two aspirin, then opted for three. She looked around the room, then in the bathroom for something to wash them down with. But before she could locate a glass, Gran bustled in with a tray of steaming tea and a plate of fancy pastries.

She babbled incomprehensibly, gesturing and pointing first to the cup, then to Hannah's head.

"Thank you." Hannah bobbed.

Gran turned down the bed, and, to Hannah's delight, she lit the fire. Hannah hadn't even realised there was a fireplace in the room. She spread her hands out towards the growing flames. The older lady patted her shoulder and headed for the door.

She said something, to which Hannah thanked her again. Then she did the strangest thing. She gestured in the air, said something, and then crossed herself.

Hannah blinked. Perhaps she was just wishing her a good sleep? Maybe some kind of evening prayer or ritual which the older woman observed?

When she was alone, Hannah took the steaming tea and sat in a large wooden chair next to the crackling fire. She sipped the tea.

"Eeww!" It was awful. Hannah gave it a sniff. It didn't smell any better than it tasted. Perhaps it was an herbal brew to help her head and that was what the gesturing towards her head had been about.

She watched the dancing flames, waiting for the tea to cool enough so she could swallow her pills. She did so then set the mug down. Her eyes fluttered as the heat relaxed her and the lapping flames mesmerised her tired eyes.

Chapter Two

Hannah awoke with a start. Her gaze darted around the room as she attempted to acclimate herself. The fire had died down some, the only other light source shone from the bathroom. Shadows danced and moved strangely around the room.

"I must have dozed off," she said to herself, straightening in the chair.

One of the shadows wavered in front of her vision and all of a sudden she had the worst feeling she wasn't alone.

Hannah tried to stand and fell over the blanket that covered her. She was positive that she hadn't covered up when she'd sat down with the tea.

She touched her forehead. Well, that must be it. Someone had been in to check on her and had covered her up. Either Jake or his gran. They were so kind.

Hannah went into the adjoining bathroom to wash and change for bed. Her head still throbbed steadily.

She looked into the mirror. "Oh, well, that's just lovely!" she said, to her bedraggled reflection. Her black mascara had run thanks to the being caught in the rain, giving her awesome racoon eyes. Her dark brown hair hung limply past her shoulders.

Turning on the hot water tap, Hannah listened to the knocking as the old pipes heated the water. She washed her face and cleaned up her eyes with the soft peach washcloth.

She pulled her T-shirt over her head and slid out of her tan capris. She looked into the mirror and admired her pink lacy bra and matching panties. She and Cass had gone shopping for all new underclothes just for this trip. They'd spent a whole day, and Hannah had bought all new bras and underwear, and even some pretty little camisoles and lingerie, just in case she landed that one-night stand. If a man was going to see her in her nothings, she was determined that they be new and pretty and feminine and lacy. She'd bought a set in every colour in the rainbow.

"Stupid Cassie!" she muttered again, cursing her friend for the hundredth time for standing her up.

Hannah wet the cloth again and began to wash her neck and arms. She washed across the top of her chest over the latest of her tattoos — the most elaborate one of the three. The same sad feeling arose that always overcame her when she looked at it.

Hannah thought back, remembering how she'd badgered Cassie into going with her to hold her hand at the tattoo parlour. She had known precisely what she was going to get when they'd walked in — an exact replica of the locket her mother had always worn. Her mother had wanted Hannah to have it, but when her mum had passed away after a long battle with cancer, Hannah hadn't been able to bring herself to remove the necklace from her. Her mum had come to Canada with that beautiful little silver locket, a gift from Hannah's father. It had travelled everywhere with her, and Hannah had wanted it to travel with her on her last journey.

That had been her plan. But when she and Cass had arrived at the tattoo parlour and Cassie had sat there going through the books, being totally annoying while Hannah waited patiently for her turn, one of the designs on the wall had captured her attention. A padlock encircled in chains, the keyhole a heart. Hannah had had the artist make one little addition that the example on the wall didn't have—a broken chain, trailing, as if the key had been lost.

Hannah had walked out with that little tattoo hovering over her left breast just above her heart, a fitting tribute to her mum. She'd always be locked away in Hannah's heart.

She sighed, looking back into the mirror as again a large shadow crossed over the door. "What *is* that?" she said squinting into the mirror.

When she peeked around the corner she couldn't see anything or anyone in the room, only the shadows that the fire created, ebbing and flowing over the walls. "Oh, get a grip," she told herself and stepped into the bedroom. "It's just the shadows flickering from the fire."

Hannah heard a noise and spun towards it. It had sounded like someone inhaling sharply. She narrowed her eyes, trying to see in the dimly lit room. There was nothing there. Feeling uncomfortable walking around in next to nothing, she pulled an oversized T-shirt from her luggage and went back into the bathroom.

Wetting the cloth with warm water again, Hannah wiped over her stomach. She felt something glide over her bare shoulder. Instead of whipping around, she stared hard into the mirror, watching for anything tangible. She brushed her hand over her shoulder. It had to have been her own hair she'd felt.

"Screw it." Tossing the washcloth into the sink, Hannah pulled the *Kiss Me, I'm Scottish* T-shirt over her bra and panties. Normally, she slept in the nude or with just a T-shirt on, but she wasn't feeling comfortable enough to do so.

She gave her teeth a quick brush and entered the bedroom again, carefully looking around. Her mind was playing tricks on her. It had been a long, weird day.

Hannah pulled on a pair of warm socks then hung her legs over the side of the bed. She worked her head from side to side, trying to relieve the knot in her neck that she believed to be the source of the headache.

Hannah heard it again. A sigh. Her head snapped up, causing pain to burst from behind her eyes. When her vision cleared, she shrieked and scrambled up onto the bed.

There was a man. At least, the portrait of a man.

"Ohh!" she breathed, as she stared at the full-length painting. The figure leaned casually on a sword. The huge frame dominated the whole wall.

Hannah slowly climbed from the bed and approached cautiously, almost waiting for something else to jump out and spook the shit out of her.

"How on earth did I not see this?" she whispered, nearing the image.

He was the most beautiful man she'd ever laid eyes on. His features were perfectly masculine and artfully aristocratic.

His eyes were dark and intense, but the artist had highlighted the inner iris with tiny white strokes, making it seem as if his eyes were lit from within. They sparkled with curiosity as though he were really seeing her. She looked into the dark orbs, holding her breath—transfixed, waiting, watching for them to shift or blink. But, of course, they remained still. She released the breath on a chuckle at her own silliness. What a marvellously talented artist to have made him look so lifelike.

She continued to examine him, noting the thick, dark hair that reached almost to the collar of his crisp-looking white shirt. She wondered if the cut was considered overlong and indecent for that time period. She tried to discern what era he might have been from, but there was nothing in the painting that even hinted at the answer. Hannah almost wished he were real. She longed to run her fingers through his thick mane. Had the artist taken liberties, or could this man have been so flawlessly designed?

"You *are* gorgeous!" She reached out almost reverently, hesitantly touching his cheek. "How could I have missed *you*?"

She allowed her eyes to drift over the rest of him. His shoulders were wide. The painter had revealed only a small glimpse of what hinted to be a gloriously muscled chest through the V of the unlaced shirt. His waist was trim but Hannah imagined there lay an amazing six-pack under the loosely tucked garment. Her eyes drifted lower, over the dark pants that covered his thick thighs, down to the calf-high, shiny black boots.

Her focus slowly lifted back over his body, her eyes lingering on his crotch for an overlong moment as she imagined that part of him, too. She didn't have to be an artisan to imagine in precise proportion to the rest of his size what a delightful handful he might be. She sighed. A girl could dream, couldn't she?

Hannah realised she was breathing rapidly. Her face was warm. Her breasts tingled. Her body was responding as it would if a real live man had captured her attention, although she couldn't ever remember having a reaction like this without some kind of stimulation first. She almost wished the swirls of paint were not cool to her touch but warm and giving, like his skin might feel.

She centred her gaze back on his amazing face, noting the high cheekbones and the strong jaw, noticing the slight cleft in his chin. She touched it, wishing that her finger could delve inside the little dent. "Oh, I like that." She smiled in appreciation of the tiny little dimple that gave the very manly features a boyish little twist.

Her attention swept to his mouth. He had full, sensual lips. "I bet you know how to kiss a girl, don't you?" she asked them, wondering what it would be like to be kissed by those lips—to be kissed by a man like him at all. Would he take a woman over? Would he dominate her until she gave in? Not like he'd have to do much convincing. Or would he seduce a woman into submission with flowery words and a soft touch? It didn't matter—either way, she'd be all over it.

Hannah swallowed hard and licked her parched lips as she ran the pad of her index finger over his full lower lip, resisting the sudden, overwhelming urge to press her own lips to the cool canvas. Hannah's body trembled.

She gave herself a mental shake. It was the first time she'd ever been turned on by a painting. Putting distance between herself and it before looking back into his dark eyes, she gasped. They didn't look as cold and intense as the first time that she'd looked into them. They were a warm chocolate brown.

"How can that be?" She exhaled, again looking to him for answers. She rubbed her eyes and looked again. She shook her head from side to side. They were back to their original cold, blank stare. Her mind was playing tricks on her.

"Maybe I'm coming down with something?" She peeked up at him once more. "Why can't I meet a man like you?" she asked him. "You know, if I did, I'd never go back home." It was the truth. There was nothing to go back home to. Her mum was gone. Cass would soon marry that idiot Paul and things would change. Again.

Hannah backed away from the portrait, switched off the bathroom light then slid into bed. She couldn't keep her eyes off the painting. The flickering firelight gave the impression that he was alive, moving.

All of a sudden, Hannah felt a moment of gripping grief, as if she mourned for the man in the painting. Her eyes filled as her chest tightened with pain. And just as fast as the feeling had come, it went, leaving her feeling nauseous and hot.

"Yeah, I'm definitely coming down with something. Just another perfect way to top off this perfect dream vacation," she mumbled, punching the pillow before snuggling deep into the covers.

Chapter Three

Hannah awoke with a start, once more feeling like she was being watched. She sat up and her eyes went immediately to the handsome man in the portrait.

"It's you, isn't it?" she accused croakily, her hand rising to her sore throat. "Oh, damn it!" she bemoaned, pushing back the heavy blankets. Her throat was on fire. She needed a drink desperately.

She stumbled back over to the fireplace and picked up the half-empty cup of tea. "I wonder if this old place has a microwave?" She wrapped the blanket that someone had been kind enough to cover her with around her shoulders.

"Come on, portrait man, show me your kitchen," she invited as she passed the painting.

She made her way carefully and quietly down the dark stairs, hoping she wouldn't wake Gran and Jake. Lightning continued to illuminate the downstairs with tiny little pulsing flashes, helping light the way.

Finding the microwave, Hannah heated the bitter tea for thirty seconds, hoping to make it warm enough to drink but not too hot. She stopped the digital counter before the appliance could beep and wake the whole house. After removing the cup, she sipped slowly. It was good enough – she drank the rest down.

"Wha…" She shuddered. "That's awful stuff." She went to the fridge and looked in, hoping to find orange juice inside, to soothe her throat. "Oh, thank you," she whispered, spotting some. She found a glass and poured herself some juice, then drank it, cooling the fire in her throat.

She touched her forehead, wondering if she were feverish. She felt very strange all of a sudden. It was like the room had taken on a life of its own. She felt and heard it breathing. It was as if she could see every particle in the room individually vibrating, moving, forming substance. Everything took on a silvery hue and wavered in front of her eyes. She leaned heavily on the counter to keep herself upright.

She was not alone.

Hannah shrieked, a strangled sound coming from her sore throat as the lightning illuminated the face of the real-life version of the man in the portrait. The blanket slipped from her shoulders. He was not far away from her. She wondered how he could have sneaked up on her like that without her hearing him. He was close enough to touch.

"It's you," she whispered. He was alive. The thought sent a thrill through her. "You scared me."

"You scared me," he repeated in a distinctive Scottish brogue. Another burst of sensation ran through her body at his accent. "You see me?"

"Barely," she rasped, more from her awareness of him than the sore throat. "It's so dark." She reached towards him. He caught her hand and guided it towards his chest, splaying her fingers against its hard warmth. His lips parted on a sigh as though he were savouring her touch. A surge of energy shot through Hannah's body as if all her molecules had suddenly come back together in one hot rush.

"You hear me?"

"Yes," she answered, wondering why he was asking her these strange questions.

"You feel me?"

"Yes," she answered, wanting to feel a whole lot more of him. He pushed her hand more solidly against his broad chest, giving her the impression he wanted it too. She moved closer, inexplicably drawn to him, just as she had been to the painting. He was even taller than she'd thought he would be. And, if possible, he was even more handsome than the artist had been able to portray. A rush of pure lust shot through her.

"It *is* you, isn't it? From the painting." She had assumed it was an old portrait, never giving thought that it might be more recent and that this glorious hunk of man might live here.

"Aye, 'tis."

He traced his thumb leisurely over her bottom lip just as she'd done to his likeness in the painting. He swept his tongue slowly across his own lip as he continued to stare down at her. She shivered with anticipation.

"Is the sayin' on your chemise the truth then, lass? Because true or no, I am goin' to kiss ya," he warned, leaning towards her.

She couldn't seem to remember her own name, let alone what her damn shirt read at that particular moment.

The minute his mouth touched hers, her body responded with a hot, liquid rush, her nipples straining against the lace covering her breasts. Her lips parted on a surprised hiss of sensation, her knees weakening as he deepened the kiss, insistently teasing her mouth open.

She clung to him, returning his kiss with growing heat. He kissed like a desperate man, a man who had no tomorrow. He broke free of her mouth and she whimpered at the loss.

He clamped a strong hand over her jaw, looking at her intensely. "You are real."

"So are you," she said, still somewhat surprised that he actually existed. She remembered the sudden bout of grief she'd endured up in her room, for a man she'd thought long dead. But he was real and he was here. And she didn't care that she didn't know one single thing about him, not even his name. It only heightened her fascination towards him. She wanted him to fuck her—no questions asked, no regrets later. She'd been turned on by just the image of him—the real thing made her burn.

She thrust both of her hands inside his shirt and was thrilled when she felt a tremor run the length of him, proof that he was just as affected as she was.

He pulled her forcibly against him, again seeking her lips. He was ravenous. Hungry. He wasn't even gentle. He devoured her, robbing her of breath. She dragged her mouth free and he cascaded kisses over her jaw, down her neck, nipping hungrily against her skin. He was intoxicating. Her head swam at the unreality of the whole situation. He was a complete stranger.

The next thing she knew, she was flat on her back on the scarred kitchen table, him moving over her. He ground his massive erection against her thigh, almost too eagerly, then he nudged her knees open with his own. Hannah protested and shifted under him.

"I'm sorry, lass, it has been a long time for me. You must remind me to be gentle."

Hannah was strangely pleased to know that he hadn't been with anyone recently. Neither had she — perhaps that explained why they were both so eager and he a little too rough.

He looked down at her, his chest heaving, waiting for her permission to continue. "Kiss me, lass." He grinned, his upper lip curving boyishly, his dark eyes dancing with mischief. "I'm Scottish."

She couldn't help but smile at the sensual yet silly invitation. How could she turn him down? She didn't need to fight the overwhelming urge to kiss him. She worked her fingers into his thick dark hair and pulled him down to her, kissing him greedily — hard and long, their tongues duelling and withdrawing.

Hannah ran her hands down his back over the wide expanse of hard muscle and coaxed him from his shirt. It looked strangely similar to the one in the painting, she thought fleetingly as he tossed it carelessly over the side of the table. She wanted to see if his chest was as amazing as she'd imagined it to be, only hinted at in the painting. She was not disappointed. His neck muscles corded with tension, tendons flexed impressively down his arms and chest as he levered himself over her. The crude-looking Celtic cross tattooed on his upper left biceps suddenly fascinated her. She dug her fingers into it, massaging the tight swell of solid strength.

"You are even more than I imagined," she whispered. "Your creator did not do you justice." She splayed her hands greedily over his skin, feeling the rich planes and dips of sinewy muscle.

He took hold of the hem of her large tee and pulled it over her head. He stilled, looking down at her. His eyes raked hotly over her tits, nicely displayed and plumped by her new bra. He massaged the side swell of her breast, his thumb hesitating above the tattoo on her chest. He leaned in and sucked on it lightly before he broke away, sending heat lancing through her. His gaze dropped lower over her flat stomach to the skimpy triangle of lace nestled between her thighs.

"What are these that you wear?" he asked, reaching out to touch the fabric as if he'd never seen the like before.

Hannah felt a little uncomfortable for a second. "They're new," she said simply, taking his hands and placing them over her breasts. He gripped her flesh firmly. She winced. He grunted another quick apology for his impatience.

Hannah placed her hands over his and squeezed softly, lifting slightly, demonstrating what she liked and the right pressure. His attention focused on their stacked palms kneading her tits. He gritted his teeth and growled. She wasn't sure if he liked being told or shown what to do, but she knew by the way his eyes blazed that he enjoyed watching.

She released her hold and he squeezed her full breasts as she'd shown him. Then he took it a step further, circling her erect nipples with his open palms, sending another hot rush of need pooling between her legs. She arched, trying to get closer. He continued exploring, caressing her body greedily, finally pausing to cup her lace-covered crotch. She thrust her hips forward, filling his hand with her tingling cunt.

Another primitive sound erupted from deep in his chest as he dove towards her, open-mouthed—he tried to nip and tongue her awakening clit right through the lace. There was no finesse, no strategy, no technique to his seduction. He wasn't quite clumsy, but he didn't seem overly concerned with her pleasure. He was caught up in his own need. But to Hannah's surprise, it didn't matter to her. She knew that it was because of her that he was on a fast track to mindless culmination, and it turned her on just knowing it. She wanted to drive him so crazy that he couldn't wait. It would give her wicked satisfaction to make a man like him come in his pants like a randy teenager before he even got to the good stuff.

She could feel the sultry heat streaming from his mouth as he exhaled heavily in excitement. The sweltering moisture and humidity wet her panties as he salivated, plastering them against her hidden pussy. Her growing arousal released its own torrent of musky liquid. The fabric worked its way into her lubricated crevice, causing the sweetest of friction under his plundering tongue. Regardless of the untamed skill, he had her hips listing underneath him. This might be a quick thing for both of them.

Belatedly, Hannah realised where they were. If he was going to continue, and it seemed like he was, they needed more privacy than the kitchen provided. God, what was she thinking? Jake or Gran could walk in at any minute.

She ran her fingers into his hair. "Let's go upstairs," she suggested.

He acted as if he hadn't heard her.

She lightly scratched his scalp with her fingernails. "Hey, how 'bout some privacy, portrait man?" She didn't know what to call him, so that would have to do.

Still, there was no response, so engrossed was he with his subject. She finally resorted to pulling his overlong hair. She reefed his head back painfully. He looked up at her dazedly for a moment before he grinned and licked his lips, like a starving man falling on a feast. The look on his face sent another thrill through her.

"Let's go upstairs before Jake or Gran walk in on us."

He watched her, puzzled for a moment, before picking her up in his arms and heading for the stairs. She felt like they were floating and before she could even clasp her arms around his neck and kiss the throbbing pulse hammering in his throat, they were in her room.

He booted the door shut, all but tossed her on the bed and fell on her, taking up right where he'd left off, his face between her legs. But it wasn't long before that wasn't enough for him. Hannah anticipated his need, because it was her own as well. There was no reason for the lace to be between them any longer now that they were alone in her room. She lifted her hips and he pulled the fabric away from her vigorously — she thought she heard it tear.

He stilled again as he looked down at her, fully exposed to his view. His breath rushed from his lungs as he groaned, another primitive but titillating sound. His mouth opened as if he were surprised. Hannah watched him, wondering at this reaction.

He then took his hands and all but framed them around her exposed flesh. He ran his fingers over her bare skin, fingering it, trying her out, touching her like a new toy. "You have no hair here," he said, sounding astounded.

Hannah was taken aback by his reaction. Her face suffused with heat, making her self-conscious. Did he not like that? She didn't think that European woman were much different from North American women anymore. Canadian boys preferred a bald beaver.

"Do you not like it this way?" she asked, apprehensively, wishing she could cover herself.

His dark eyes shot to hers. "I...I've never seen the like," he breathed. His smouldering gaze warmed her as she saw the raw pleasure return to his gaze. He looked down at her, and his nostrils flared as he groaned in rapture, licking his lips. He lunged at her, much like he'd done on the kitchen table. He kissed her bare mound slowly and tenderly, as she would expect him to kiss her mouth. It felt strangely intimate and erotic.

"How did ya accomplish this?" he asked, his breath heaving. "'Tis lovely. You are so smooth and soft." He skimmed his closed lips everywhere, all over her, his unshaven jaw rasping against her bare skin, making her shudder with sensitivity.

She chuckled. "It's magic."

He stilled and his gaze shot to hers. "Are ya a witch?"

She laughed uneasily. "No, but I've been called something similar a time or two." She thrust her hands into his hair and pulled her knees back, opening herself to him, and he continued his exploration.

"By the Christ, lass, ya taste of sweet honey," he groaned, then finally swept his tongue over the hot, wet opening begging for his attention. He licked through the slickness leading straight to her delicate clit, a deep sound of approval rumbling through his chest. He probed and sucked the sensitive bud almost painfully.

"Not so rough," she admonished.

"I'm sorry, I can't help it," he murmured, taking up a much softer stroke with his tongue.

"Mmm," she moaned, encouraging this new method. "Ahh, yes!" she purred as she felt the first stirrings of orgasm uncurling deep inside her. "Swirl your tongue clockwise," she panted, wriggling her backside, straining to increase the pressure now. He hesitated. Again, she wondered if he didn't appreciate her telling him what she liked, but she was too far gone to give a shit about his delicate ego at the moment. She slid her hand down between them, pausing to slip the tip of her finger between his damp lips, effectively lubricating it. She began to demonstrate for him what she wanted him to do with his tongue.

He watched — stunned, she thought — before being mesmerised by her caressing the engorged bud. Circling fast then slow, one way then the other, creating delicious friction before flicking over her clit quickly, simulating what she wanted him to do to her. She tapped the nub lightly and started again. She trembled at the sensation of not only the raw heat she was producing for herself, but also the almost wicked feeling it gave her to have him watching her do it. She could feel his hot breath escalating as his excitement grew, creating a tantalising sensation fanning across her exposed flesh.

He snarled again, an animalistic primitive sound, knocking her hand away with a swat of his own. He lapped and teased just as she wanted.

Hannah's muscles bunched and flexed as she strained to drag it out. Now that he'd finally got the rhythm, it felt so incredibly good — she wanted it to last a little longer. Her hands fisted and her toes curled as she tried to prolong the sweet suffering.

She could feel the mattress rise and fall as he thrust his hips into it in his own enthusiasm. *Oh, save some for me*, she thought, realising that earlier she'd been praying for him to come, just to give herself some cheap thrill to overwhelm a guy who was clearly out of her league, like her portrait man. But now she wanted to be the beneficiary of his rock-hard cock plunging into her and not the mattress, which was the only thing profiting from his furious thrusting.

But she was too late — he groaned deep in his throat and she felt his body shudder. The mattress began a slower roll under her hips as he ground into it, sustaining his climax.

He slowed his tongue's frenzied pace on her clit, to her disappointment. But even that was short-lived when he again started kissing her pussy as he had kissed her mouth. Deep sounds of satisfaction reverberated through his chest, making his lips vibrate with a low hum, sending Hannah into a quivering orgasm of her own.

Her back arched as she came, but instead of backing off, as she wanted him to do, he kept up the assault with his lips and tongue. She felt much too sensitive to go on — it no longer felt good. She needed some distance. She tried to wiggle away but he seized her hips roughly, holding her right where she was. He was so strong.

"Stop," she said, trying to push his head away.

"No, I want more!" he demanded loudly, pushing back using his muscular neck to get what he wanted.

She attempted to close her legs but he forced them wide, planting his big hands on her thighs.

"Please...stop!" she cried. "You're hurting me!"

He stilled immediately. "I'm sorry," he said before laying his head on her bare stomach. "You are like no one I have ever known before. You are so beautiful. So open. You must forgive me, I have no control."

He said all the right things. She closed her hands around his head, holding him to her. He turned his face and kissed her stomach, slowly making his way up to her shoulders.

He grinned down at her, playfully. "We did not remove this." He ran a finger down the inside of her bra strap, his thumb again covering her tattoo, making her shiver at his touch. "But we have time, yeah?"

She nodded.

The corner of his mouth lifted cockily. "So what's the verdict, lass? Do I know how to kiss?"

"You *were* watching me!" she accused.

"Aye, ya knew that I was. You could feel it. You could feel me. And you liked it," he finished self-assuredly.

"How would you know that?"

"The same way that I know you wanted to kiss me, even when you thought that I wasna real. I could see it in your eyes. How you forced yourself to turn from me."

"Because it was just the portrait. The real thing is much better." She ran her hand over his chest.

"Ya are a bold one, aren't ya?"

She shrugged. "I don't know that it's bold to know what I like or what I want. It just makes it better for both of us, don't you think?"

"Aye. Although I am not used to such a thing. Where I come from the man is the aggressor and the women sometimes just...lie there." He lifted a shoulder.

"A woman's pleasure is just...what? Secondary? Where do you come from, the Dark Ages?" She chuckled, then winced remembering her sore throat. "Where I come from a woman's pleasure is just as important as a man's. And I will have you know that from what I've seen, a man's pleasure is only heightened when he knows that he has pleasured the woman." She wrapped her hand around her aching throat. Funny, it hadn't bothered her at all while she was busy with him.

"You are ill."

"Perhaps I shouldn't have kissed you. You might get sick too."

"I doubt that. I will get you some cordial," he offered, rolling out of bed.

"Cordial?" she questioned. "Oh, you mean juice. Thank you." Just as he reached the door, she remembered their clothing left in the kitchen. "Will you pick up our shirts and the blanket before someone else finds them?"

He nodded as he disappeared.

Hannah sighed and raised her arms over her head to stretch. What a strange turn her trip had taken now. After all the misery she'd endured yesterday, she had been convinced she should go home, and now that was the furthest thing from her mind. She might not even continue on to Scotland or Ireland, but spend what time she had left here, if Gran didn't mind her staying on. She'd pay or work or both.

She unhooked her bra and tossed it over the side of the bed, then pulled the covers over her naked body, waiting sleepily for him to return.

Chapter Four

She was almost asleep when she felt that strange shift of time and space again. She could see every jittering particle that made up the room. Then he was there, appearing as though he'd just stepped out of the portrait and not come through the door. Hannah shook her head, trying to clear it. She must be feverish. She touched her cheek. It did feel warm.

He set the glass of juice on the table beside her and sat down on the edge of the bed. Hannah stared up at him and admired his chiselled features. He was so handsome that he didn't seem real. How could anyone be so heavenly?

"You are lookin' at me like that again." His mouth curved cockily. "I am — what did ya say? — gorgeous."

"And arrogant too," Hannah retorted, sitting up to take a sip of the orange juice. He ran a finger over the blue maple leaf on her right wrist. She kept her left hand over the sheet, keeping herself covered. "Ahh, that's good. Thank you. It feels so good on my throat."

"You ink your skin," he commented.

"So do you," she said.

"Where I come from this is another thing women do not do."

"Where do you come from, Caveman?" she teased.

He ignored her question, staring at her bare shoulders, his eyes warming by degrees. He traced his index finger from just under her ear, softly following the column of her throat, over her shoulder, causing goosebumps to skitter over her skin.

"I would have liked to have removed that garment from you." His husky voice went right through her. His speech was somewhat formal, she noted, wondering where it was that he came from, but she didn't ask again. Not yet. She liked this air of anonymity. It was exhilarating and felt somehow naughty.

She smiled. "We have time, yeah?" she asked, using his line from earlier, hoping that he too wanted to spend more time with her. They'd have time to talk and get to know one another when this sizzling sexual energy was not so raw.

"Aye, but I would not waste it," he said, tugging the sheet from her grasp, exposing her breasts to him.

His gaze dropped, lingering on her tits. A ragged growl escaped his lips as he moved onto the bed, stalking her. He threw a big knee over her so that he straddled her legs. He placed big hands over her boobs and he cupped and plumped them just as she'd schooled him earlier in the night. She slid down the bed onto her back, coaxing him with her. She guided his jaw, persuading his warm lips back to hers. Hannah kissed him with utter abandon. She was feeling so reckless with this guy. It was crazy but at the same time such an aphrodisiac to be with a stranger. She'd never done this before—it made her bolder, and she kissed him all open-mouthed and unrefined, as he seemed to like it.

He was very vocal as his excitement grew, groaning and growling. Hannah worried that Gran or Jake might hear them. What kind of impression would that make? She was a guest in their home shagging...the help? Maybe he worked here for Gran, or maybe he was a family member? Which would be worse? Whoever he was, he was a guy she'd barely exchanged a few words with and knew absolutely nothing about except that he was Scottish, he liked to kiss like there was no tomorrow and that the women he dated apparently didn't wear pretty undies or keep their privates well maintained. And he very much enjoyed slobbering over said privates.

He slid his mouth from hers and moved over her breasts. He went straight to her nipples, sucking and nipping her crudely. She tried moving around under him to make it better for herself but it wasn't helping.

He raised his dark head and looked at her as if he knew he was not pleasing her, his dark orbs blazing desire. "You will show me what you like. I would pleasure my woman to pleasure myself."

Hannah trembled as he called her his woman. No one had ever called her that.

"Okay, buster, you asked for it." She not so gently coaxed him onto his back.

"Buster?" he questioned.

"Right, for now, I'm Lass and you're Buster." No names needed.

He gave her a slow, bemused nod.

She ignored him. "Can we get rid of these?" She ran a finger on the inside of his pants. "They are kind of in my way." He untied the laces. She watched, fascinated by the fact that he had lace-up trousers at all—

authentic-looking apparel just like he'd worn to pose for the portrait. Perhaps he worked at a Renaissance house or a medieval tourist attraction, she thought momentarily, trying to explain his clothing.

Then Hannah's attention went straight to the impressive, mouth-watering bulge in those breeches, and all the questions she had didn't seem to matter.

"Ya have a difficult time keepin' your eye from there, yeah?" he teased her.

She felt the blush creep up her neck.

"I saw how your eyes lingered. Ya wondered, didn't ya?" He pulled the tight-fitting material from his body. "I promise ya, lass, ya will not be disappointed," he vowed arrogantly.

His cock sprang free, and she was not disappointed but again riveted. He was uncircumcised. She'd never been with a guy who hadn't had the procedure. This was a night of firsts. She reached for him but he sidestepped her.

"If ya be wantin' me to last, lass, ya had better show me what you want and hurry up aboot it."

"Then on your back, portrait man. School's in," she quipped.

When he was on his back, she settled herself on top of him.

"You are so soft, so smooth," he moaned.

She swished her body over him sensually, demonstrating how very soft she was all over. He looped his arms around her back, his palms skating over her skin. She started kissing him, teasing his lips. She kissed his chin, even running the tip of her tongue through that little cleft that captured her attention. She lightly grazed it with her teeth before moving lower, kissing, nipping, gently sucking his neck and chest.

She wrapped her hands around his pecs and squeezed them softly. Using her open palms, she ringed his tiny nipples, as he'd done to her. They stiffened at her touch. She'd never stimulated a man's before. She was trying many new things tonight. She felt powerful and eager to please him. It was just as potent to demonstrate exactly how he could satisfy her by using him as the example.

Hannah plucked each bud at the same time, making sure that they were fully erect. She looped around each one slowly with her fingers, even scraping them lightly with her fingernails.

He exhaled heavily and surged, grinding his hot, distended cock against her. She sneaked a peek up at him. His head was thrown back, his eyes closed, his mouth open in gratification.

She alternated kissing then licking the hardened peaks, with feathery, teasing strokes. His chest rumbled with pleasure. She loved the noises he made.

Hannah circled his right side with her tongue, making sure to duplicate the same motion on his left with the tip of her index finger. He roared and almost came off the bed. She knew how good that felt.

"Ssshhh!" Hannah hissed. "Shut up, they'll hear us!" she admonished, cupping her hand over his mouth.

He grunted, grasping either side of her head and pushing her back towards his chest. Hannah grinned, pleased by his reaction. She repeated the action, swirling in tandem with her tongue and her finger, gliding both deliciously over the raised flesh. She even used her teeth to give him the softest little nip before rotating faster and faster while keeping in sync. Stirring and stroking, lapping and twiddling. That was the way that she liked it. It always gave her the feeling that two tongues were involved in loving her.

"Doesn't it feel good?" she asked him. "Wouldn't you like two women to suckle you at the same time?" Not that she would share. He was hers.

He roared again, his hips surging against her.

She was almost as stimulated as she would be if he were doing this to her. Her cunt was burning with insatiable eagerness and dripping wet. She rubbed her glistening pussy over his thigh, demanding the pressure, as she continued to demonstrate what she liked.

His chest hummed with one solid moan after another.

Hannah soon forgot all about the tutorial. She just did whatever felt good. And it *all* felt good. Her heart was pounding—she could barely breathe. She wanted his tongue on her clit doing all the magical things that she was now doing to him. Imagining it sweeping over the aching bud, she began a fast, flicking rhythm on his nipple that would have brought her to climax instantly.

"Oh, God!" she moaned, dragging her wet, throbbing pussy over his leg, riding it. A tiny spasm fluttered deep inside her. He flexed his thigh as she moved over him, making the muscle hard for her. She was like a cat and he was the scratching post. She wanted him inside her. And she wanted it now.

She sat up and grasped his quivering cock firmly in her hand. She rose up on her knees over him, rubbing the head of his unaltered penis between her swollen, saturated lips then slowly squatted over him. She closed her eyes in rapture as she sank down the length of his hot, straining flesh. She sighed in near relief to finally having him filling her.

He bellowed, attempting to sit up, throwing his arms around her. He stilled and she knew that he was trying to stop himself from coming, trying to prolong this exquisite feeling. He was so strong she couldn't move. She could feel his cock jerking and rippling inside her. She knew that he wouldn't be maintaining that impressive stiffness for much longer and she wanted to ride before he lost all substance.

"Ahh, let me move," she begged. She pushed at his chest forcefully, making him take to his back again. He stared at her in surprise. But at the moment she didn't care if he didn't like aggressive women. That was what he was about to experience, and when she was done with him, he'd be changing his 'type'.

She planted her hands in the middle of his chest and she used her leg muscles, pumping her tightening pussy up and down his turgid cock. Throwing her head back, she concentrated on one thing—her own climax—knowing that hers would bring his. She rode him hard, wringing every last ounce of juice from them both. She shuddered, small cries of ecstasy ringing from her parched throat as one gripping, delectable wave after another pounded through her. She ground herself against him until every last delicious tremor subsided then she collapsed against his sweaty chest until her breathing returned to normal.

Perhaps she was not so different, she thought. She'd been obsessed in seeking her own pleasure and his had been secondary. She gave a mental shrug. He'd seemed to enjoy it anyway.

She took a deep, satisfied breath and attempted to roll off him. "Do not leave me," he said gruffly, grabbing her wrist and shifting his hips to keep them connected.

"I was just moving off you. I'm not going anywhere."

His dark eyes searched hers and he relaxed his hold on her. They shifted onto their sides as he slipped out of her. She saw disappointment cross his handsome face.

She smiled sleepily, happy that he seemed to want to spend more time with her, too. She rubbed her thumb over his cheek. "We have time," she whispered, cuddling into his arms. He tucked her head under his chin and held her. She was asleep within seconds.

Chapter Five

Hannah liked sleeping with him. Every time she moved, he touched her in some way, running his hands over her, reassuring her that he was there. He kissed her gently on the forehead or on the cheek, occasionally on the lips. He was so sweet and attentive. She could honestly get used to this. She wanted to turn into him and do it again, but she was so hot and groggy from whatever she was coming down with that she couldn't seem to find the energy. She'd make it up to him in the morning, she promised herself, before falling back into a disturbed sleep.

Later, she awoke—slowly, but she knew immediately that she was alone, his warm chest no longer under her ear. She stretched, aching all over. Her throat felt less raw, but was an annoying dull pain that she knew would plague her throughout the day. She opened her eyes and tucked her hands behind her head so that she could stare at his portrait in the light of day. "Good morning, handsome," she greeted him before hopping out of bed and heading for the bathroom.

Hannah enjoyed a long, hot shower. Wrapping one towel around her wet hair and another around her body, she stepped out of the stall. She wiped the steam from the mirror and looked at her reflection. She was a little pale, like she got when she was sick. She entered the bedroom and ransacked her luggage for some clothes. She let the terrycloth drop to the floor and looked over her shoulder at the portrait. "That's for you, if you're watching," she chuckled, going back into the bathroom.

It wasn't until Hannah pulled her camisole over her head that she noticed the bruises around her breasts. *Somebody's* overeager fingerprints marred her pale flesh.

Strutting back into the bedroom in just the camisole and panties, Hannah hoped to lure him out from wherever it was that he'd been spying on her. But, to her disappointment, he didn't come. She finished dressing, pulled her damp hair into a sloppy bun, and went in search of her portrait man.

Hannah found Jake and his gran in the kitchen having breakfast, but was disappointed that the face she sought was not at the table awaiting her.

Gran turned and gave Hannah a weak greeting before turning back to the pot she was stirring.

"G'morning, Hannah, did you sleep well?" Jake asked, spooning a mouthful of what looked and smelt like porridge into his mouth.

Jake smiled at her. Hannah wondered if he'd heard their rather noisy sex during the night and a blush suffused her cheeks.

"Yes, thank you," she said, unable to look directly at him. She pulled out a chair and sat down. "Do you have to work today?" she enquired.

"Not in town, no. But I have chores I need to do on the farm. But, whenever you like, I can run you back into town to catch that bus to Swansea."

"Well...um..." She bit her lip. They were going to think she was a pushy bitch but she wanted to stay, if they didn't mind. "Do you think...um, well, do you think your gran would mind if I stuck around for a couple of days? I'll pay, just like I would at any hotel. I can work, do chores for her, or help you, if you'd like. You might have to show me what to do. I've never worked on a farm before, but I'm willing to learn." She looked at him hopefully.

He said a mouthful of Welsh to his gran who turned from the counter and stared hard at Hannah, speaking to Jake quickly. "I'm guessing she'd rather I not stay?" she asked Jake.

"No, it's not that," Jake answered, not looking at Hannah. "You're welcome to stay if that's what you'd like to do. Gran just thinks that you might be more comfortable, you know, at Gorman's in Swansea, like you planned."

That was a less than enthusiastic invitation. Well, maybe she'd just stay for one more day and convince portrait guy to come and stay in Swansea with her. He could still go to work and do the things he had to do then spend the rest of his time with her. Maybe she'd forget all about going on to Scotland and Ireland. She might just spend the rest of her trip with him if he were game.

Gran set a hot steaming cup of tea in front of Hannah. "Thank you," she said, hoping it wasn't the same blend as last night. She took a tentative sniff and smiled when it smelt of real tea. She took a small sip.

"How's the headache?"

"Mmm, better, thanks. Just have a bit of a sore throat today."

"Gran says you look a little flushed."

Hannah chuckled nervously.

Jake's gran set a bowl of porridge in front of her and sat down to join them.

Hannah took a spoonful of treacle from the fancy little pot and swirled it over the porridge, wondering how to bring up the subject of her missing man. She really should have got his name before she fell asleep. It would make this enquiry a lot easier.

"Um…" She tried the oatmeal. "Do you have…workers—you know, employees that work here—besides you?"

"Nope, there's just me and Gran. When we need outside help, the neighbours usually pitch in."

"Huh. Do you rent out rooms?" she fished.

"Nope, only to you." He chuckled, scraping the last of his breakfast from the bottom of the bowl.

Hannah pinched her lip. "Um, okay, look… Last night, I, uh… My throat was sore, as I said, so I came down here to see if maybe you had some orange juice. I hope you don't mind," Hannah rushed. "Um, and I, uh, ran into a man…"

Jake's Gran shot to her feet and she crossed herself just like she'd done last evening before she left Hannah's room.

"You met a man…down here?" Jake said slowly.

Hannah swallowed and laughed again uneasily. "Yeah, he…um…he was here in the kitchen. He looks just like the guy in the painting in my room."

Jake's eyes rounded and his spoon fell noisily to the table as his gran spoke rapidly in an overly excited voice. Uneasiness skittered across the back of Hannah's neck.

"Did he give you a name?" Jake asked. "Gran wants to know."

"No, I didn't catch his name. I was hoping you would tell me his name."

Jake shook his head. "Nope, I can't help you." He stood up from the table and took his bowl to the sink. "You let me know when you're ready to go to the bus station, Hannah. I'll gladly take you."

"But...I was hoping...to stay and..."

Jake shook his head slowly with a sceptical look on his young face. "And hang out with a ghost some more? I doubt that's what you had in mind for your holiday."

"A ghost?" She gave a half-assed chuckle, watching Jake intently. "Right, a ghost. Funny. Canadian tourist, right here"—she pointed at her own face—"in haunted old Wales," she tried to joke, but by the look on his face he didn't find it funny.

"Look, Hannah, I don't know what to say. Gran swears he's here. I've never actually seen him, so I don't really believe it, but I will admit some strange stuff goes on here that defies explanation. If you ran into him last night, I'm sorry that he scared you."

"He didn't...scare me... *You're* scaring me. You're trying to make me believe that...that the guy I"—she almost said 'fucked' before she caught herself—"met was a ghost?"

"Well, I guess you should consider yourself lucky that he didn't frighten you. I've gotta go get some work done before you need to leave."

He began to walk out of the room. Hannah jumped up and gripped his arm as near hysteria climbed up her sore throat. "The guy, in the portrait. He's dead?"

"Well, I don't know. I assume he is. That painting has been here as long as I can remember. It was here when Gran was a child, she told me before. Her family has lived here for generations."

Hannah began to tremble uncontrollably. Jake lowered her into a chair.

"It's okay, Hannah. You'll be all right. I'll get you out of here. I'll take you to Swansea and you can just carry on with your trip. Just think of the story you'll get to tell when you get back to Canada."

The story she'd get to tell? Who the hell would believe her? *Oh, by the way, Cass, I shagged a ghost while I was in the UK.* They'd lock her up and throw away the key for sure. "But…but who is the man in the painting?" She looked at him, needing answers.

"I don't know. Like I said, it was here. For all we know it is just an artist's vision and not a real person at all." He looked over at his gran and shrugged.

Hannah didn't believe that. He had been real. If he was a—she didn't even want to think it—a ghost, then he had to have been alive at some point.

Hannah felt near to tears. She covered her mouth with her hand trying to keep it in. What was going on? She felt that same awful ache of grief she'd experienced upstairs. She couldn't be so sick that she'd hallucinated this whole thing.

Jake bent down and patted her shoulder. "Why don't you go throw some water on your face and pack up your things? I'll take you to your hotel."

Hannah swallowed hard and nodded, getting up and stumbling blindly towards the stairs.

She entered the room, keeping her back to the portrait, piling her things into her suitcase without folding them neatly. She went into the bathroom and turned on the faucet, throwing cold water on her face then drying it without even looking into the mirror, afraid that she might see him there.

Hannah had to know. She pulled the collar of her shirt wide and looked down at her breasts. The bruises were still there. *What the fuck? Wow, I've been 'used' by a ghost.* Leave it to her to have a relationship with the most unavailable guy around. *Oh, wait — he wasn't a guy at all.* She felt light-headed. Jake was right, she needed to get the hell away from here.

Hannah took her toothbrush and hairbrush from the sink, tossed them carelessly into the case, and zipped it up. Hastily, she looked around the room for anything that she might have forgotten.

"Can I help...?"

Hannah jumped a mile at the sound of Jake's voice.

"I'm sorry," he apologised. "I just wanted to help with your bags."

"Thank you," she whispered. Allowing him to take the two bigger bags, she followed him out, slinging her carry-on over a shoulder. As Hannah passed the painting she had to expend an enormous amount of willpower not to look at it. It was as if it pulled at her, demanding her attention. She ignored it and hurried down the stairs after Jake.

As Hannah reached the bottom of the stairs the floor tilted. The room's particles whizzed around and she knew he was near. Even though it felt like she was going to pass out or throw up, she beelined for the exit. Hannah pulled open the massive door and lunged outside, inhaling deep gulps of cool air into her lungs.

She sat down heavily on the front steps while Jake put her things in the car.

"You ready, Hannah?" he asked, looking down at her.

"Yes."

He reached a hand out to her and she took it gratefully, needing some support — not only physically but emotionally as well.

They drove down the lane. Hannah had already made the decision that she wouldn't look back. But she did, and almost choked when she saw an old farmhouse. Last night when they'd driven up, it had been a castle. She'd seen it. The lightning had flashed and she'd seen a castle. At least that was what she'd thought. Nothing was making sense. As she stared at the old house, she caught sight of movement at the very topmost, octagonal-shaped window in what must be an attic. The pane of glass took on the silvery hue she'd witnessed so many times during the night, as if the house or someone in it were trying to summon her.

Hannah closed her eyes and turned back around in the seat.

Chapter Six

"Seriously, Hannah, it's no trouble. And, honestly, the way you look right now, I'd feel a whole lot better if you'd just let me drive you to Swansea myself."

"No, Jake, please just take me to the bus terminal. You've already gone above and beyond for me. And I know I'm taking away time from your chores. Please just take me there."

"Well, okay. If that's what you'd prefer...but I really don't mind. I..."

She shook her head and he paused.

"You don't believe that shit, do you?" he asked her.

"I don't know what I believe at the moment. You said yourself things go on in your house that you can't explain. Who knows?"

They rode in silence until he pulled up in front of the bus station. The bus was already there. Jake jumped out, retrieved her luggage and handed it over to the driver, who promptly stashed it in the undercarriage.

Hannah got out more slowly with her carry-on. She handed her ticket to the bus driver.

"Well, Hannah, I've certainly enjoyed meeting you. I hope once you get home and have time to look back on this, you'll not think of me as the guy that lured you to the haunted house."

She attempted a smile. "I don't think that." She leaned over and hugged him. When she pulled away, he blushed, shoving his hands into his pockets.

Hannah undid the little red maple leaf pin from her jacket and pinned it to Jake's denim one. "Thank you for everything. The Welsh are the kindest people I know and I will take out an ad in the *Toronto Sun* when I get home letting everyone know it." She smiled at the boy and stepped onto the bus.

"Thank your gran for me." Hannah realised she'd been in such a rush to escape the house that she hadn't even shown her gratitude to the older woman for taking her in when they could have just as easily dropped her at a hotel. Now she wished they had. Maybe when she got back home she would send them a nice gift basket to thank them for their kindness. "Goodbye, Jakob."

Hannah settled herself onto the bus and waved at Jake while it pulled away.

She looked around. There were only a few other passengers, all engrossed in newspapers or their cell phones or iPads. Hannah leaned her forehead against the glass and finally gave in to the tears that had been dogging her since she'd left Jake's kitchen.

How could she have been so…so…? What was the word for being suckered by a spirit? How could she have not known there was something off about the whole thing? Seriously—what would a man like him see in her? *Man.* He wasn't even a man. But he'd felt like a man. His skin had been warm to the touch like a man. He'd reacted as a man would. Yes, his speech had been strange, his reactions to her personal habits a little awkward. The clothes that he wore were different than anything she'd ever seen. But a ghost? Really? No. It was just too crazy to accept. He had a pulse—she'd seen it beating in his neck. He had a heartbeat—she'd heard it thumping in his chest under her ear while she slept. He had muscles that flexed and blood that ran through his veins. He had come inside her. She'd felt it. She'd washed it away this morning in the shower.

But what about that strange molecular disturbance that occurred whenever he entered a room? What the hell was that? And why would a ghost even want to fuck, or need it? How could a spirit even do that with a human? He'd bruised her skin, for crying out loud! If she'd known he was a ghost, she never would have let him go all the way!

Hannah shook her head at that silly argument. Dear God, why was she even wasting her time trying to figure this out?

Her head was beginning to pound again. When she got to Swansea, she'd find a drugstore and buy some over-the-counter cold medicine and sleep for the entire day. And tomorrow, she would make arrangements and go the fuck home. She felt nauseous, as if the bus were shaking, weaving back and forth.

"Ya said if ya ever met a man like me, ya wouldna leave," came the all too familiar brogue she was trying to forget. It wasn't queasiness she'd been feeling.

This couldn't be happening. She was hallucinating for sure. Her fever was so high that it had affected her mind. When she opened her eyes there would be no one there.

She opened her eyes and turned her head towards the voice. She could see him. He was shirtless, of all things, riding the bus in the seat across the aisle from her.

"I didn't meet *a man*, now did I?" she retorted.

He had the decency to look away and look properly contrite. "I am a man. I think I proved that to ya, lass."

"You took advantage of me. You lied to me."

The man in the seat just up from her looked back at her wide-eyed. "I did no such thing," he said, in yet another accent. She had no idea where the hell he was from and she didn't care.

"I wasn't talking to you," she snapped.

He looked around the back of the bus.

"Let me guess. *He* can't see you," she said looking straight at the man/ghost haunting her.

"Do you think I'd go out in public without being dressed properly, lass, if other people could see me?"

"So then why did you come out without a shirt?"

He grinned. "Well, I knew that you preferred me without, and I thought it might help my cause."

"What cause? And how would you know if I preferred you without your shirt?"

"Admit it. Ya do."

Her lips tightened and her eyes moved over his well-muscled—if long-dead—chest. "What cause?" she demanded through gritted teeth.

"I would apologise for—"

"For lying to me, for taking advantage of me—"

"Oh, I think there was mutual takin' advantage of, lass. Ya took what ya wanted from me too."

"I didn't hear you complaining," she thundered.

"And I didn't hear you complainin', either, lass."

"Ohhh, just go away!" she barked. The man ahead got up out of the seat and moved even farther away from her, giving her strange looks as he did so.

She closed her eyes and tried to clear her mind, thinking she could just make him go away if she ignored him.

The next thing she knew, her friendly phantom was pulling at the button on her capris.

She swatted at his hands. "What the hell do you think you're doing? Stop that!"

Everyone on the bus turned and looked at her. "Is there a problem?" the bus driver asked, looking back through the long rear-view mirror.

Hannah held up her palm. "No, no problem," she replied weakly.

"Let me touch you, lass. Then you'll believe that I'm real."

"You are not real!"

"Then let me touch you because I very much enjoyed what you have hidden in your trews. It is real for me."

"Drop dead!" she snarled before she thought.

"You're about four hundred years too late for that, lass."

The air in the bus warbled and he was gone. Four hundred years? 1612? What on earth had cut his life short? And when had she begun to believe that this could possibly be real?

* * * *

It wasn't a particularly long ride to Swansea. Hannah got off the bus, with all the other passengers staring at her as if she had three heads. Even the bus driver made sure that he didn't touch her when he passed her the bags, as if her craziness might rub off on him.

She sighed heavily. "Gorman's?"

The bus driver pointed and she slogged down the street in that direction, dragging her suitcases.

Hannah checked in and went straight to her room. She called down to room service and asked if they had any kind of concierge service, hoping someone else would go to the drugstore for her. There was no concierge, but as Hannah had found, the Welsh were very friendly and the woman at the desk said she would send something up to help with the cold symptoms she was suffering.

She waited until that arrived. The nice woman at the desk had also sent a tray of juice and tea and ginger ale and various sweet pastries. Hannah then ran herself a nice bath, sank into the hot scented bubbles and promptly began to cry again.

She felt like she was going to puke and didn't even need to open her wet eyes to know that he was there.

"Please don't cry. I didn't mean to make you sad, lass."

"Go away!"

"You don't mean that. You have questions and so do I. Can't you just be civil with me until we both get what we need?"

She looked up at him and crossed her arms. "So, start talking, then go away!" He'd at least donned a shirt this time, she noted.

"Let's start with your name, English."

"I'm Canadian."

"Can-a-dian," he said it slowly. "That is a strange name, lass."

"*No!*" She swatted the water, sending bubbles flying. "I'm from Canada. My name is Hannah. Are you a stupid ghost?"

"Mmm, Hannah, I like that. It suits you. And, no, I do not believe I am unintelligent. Perhaps your country did not exist in my time or if it did, I had no way of knowing of it."

He had a point there. "What is your name?" she asked, grudgingly.

"Lockhart."

She should have known that he would have an exotic sounding name.

"Is that a surname?"

"No. That would be Munro."

"And from whence do you hail, Lockhart Munro?" she asked snidely.

"Airdrie."

"Why are you haunting Jake and Gran's house?"

"I don't really haunt anything. I just am."

She rolled her eyes.

"I don't," he insisted, coming to kneel beside the tub so that they were almost eye level. "No one has ever seen me, until you."

"Yeah, right—that's why Jake's Gran crosses herself every time she passes the painting."

"I'll admit—I move things around just to play with her. I never said I wasn't mischievous. What else is there to do? She stops and listens and she curses the air but never once has she caught a glimpse of me. That's why I was so stunned when you saw me. But not only did you see me, you could touch me and hear me. Do you know how long I've waited, lass— Hannah—to feel another's touch again? I have dreamt of it and when you touched me, I wanted to touch for as long as I was allowed to enjoy the gift. I could feel it when you were touching the painting. I felt you the minute you set foot in that house."

Okay, he was getting to her. She reached out and tangled her wet fingers with his.

"I have never experienced it before — not since I was cursed to the painting."

"Cursed to the painting? You actually walked out of that painting. I really did see that?"

He nodded.

"You live in there?"

"I exist in there."

"Are you dead?"

"I'm not entirely sure whether I am dead or in some kind of limbo, or some kind of hell. It is just part of the curse. It took me some time to even realise that I could step out of the portrait. And then, by the time that I could do so, I was no longer in my home. I was in — Gran's? Is that what you call her? — I was in her home. A stranger's home."

"What made you realise that you could come out?"

"I got angry. I was losing my mind. I wanted out. Whatever escape that could be provided. Death. An end to it. If I could kill myself just to end the loneliness, I would do so. So I began ranting and raving, cursing at the world and to God, and the next thing I knew, I was standing in the bedroom you were housed in. So, I play with the people that live there. Perhaps it is wrong, but it is what it is."

"So you've been there in that house for four hundred years?"

"I don't know how long I have been there. But I have been cursed that long."

"Have you ever left that house?"

"No. I did try many times to follow Jake's grandmother out of the house, even when she was a child, but I never could. Not until you."

"So, this is the first time you've ever been this far away from the portrait?"

"Aye. I can feel its pull even now. I am resisting it."

She was well aware of its magnetism, but *he* was the lure for her, not the painting.

"How were you able to get out of the house today then?"

"I ranted and raved again."

"What were you ranting and raving about today?"

"You."

"Me?" she questioned.

"You left. The one woman—of all the people who have passed through that house—that could see me, hear me, touch me. I could talk to her, touch her, and, miracle upon miracles, I could make love to her. And God, or the world or hell or whatever all this is, would dare to take her away from me? You said you would stay. You said that if you met a man like me you would not leave. Do you know what it did you me to see you so distraught and disbelieving, then driving away?" The pain and accusation in his eyes was almost more than she could bear. "I couldn't even explain. You were gone. I thought to never see you again, and I would spend the rest of this miserable existence alone." A tear escaped his eye and he brushed it away quickly then stared at the wetness.

"That hasn't happened before, either?" she asked.

He shook his head. "You are the key." She shivered at his words. "Don't you see? All this is happening now, for a reason. You are my saviour. You can break the curse for me. You can set me free."

"But what if I can't?" She looked up at him doubtfully.

He shrugged a broad shoulder. "It is more than I have ever known before. And even if we do not succeed, at least we will have tried."

"What will break the curse?"

"I need you to take the portrait home."

"Home?"

"To my home. To Trafalis Hall in Airdrie."

"Why?"

"I'm not sure." He again rolled a shoulder at the strangeness of it. "I just feel that I need to be home."

A horrible thought occurred to her. "Lockhart." She said his name softly and his dark eyes came to hers. "What if…?" She almost hated to say it, not wanting the hope that she could see in his eyes dim. "What if this Trafalis Hall no longer exists? It has been four hundred years. I went to find my mother's childhood home and it is no longer there, and that has only been a handful of decades."

"I have to try, Hannah. *We* have to try."

"Do you think Gran will let the painting go?"

He snorted. "She'll probably give it to you to be rid of me." His grin made him irresistible. Her gaze settled on his full lips. "You are lookin' at me in that way again, Hannah-lass." He'd bent his head to kiss her, when all of sudden she felt sick.

"Oh, Lockhart, you're going to go!"

"I know, lass…" He barely spoke before he was snatched from her side.

Hannah dried off as quickly as she could, packed her things and then called a taxi. Screw the expense—she needed that portrait.

Chapter Seven

"I need the painting," Hannah pleaded with Jake. "I know this sounds strange and I know you think I'm nuts, but not as much as your gran, apparently." Hannah hazarded a sidelong glance at the older woman, who stood with her arms crossed, glaring at her.

Hannah decided to plead right to the source, but before she could, she felt the sure-fire signs that Lockhart had just inserted himself into the space.

"Are ya all right, Hannah lass?" She heard his deep voice. She nodded slightly for his benefit. "Ya seem to have an adverse reaction to my comin' and goin'."

"Gran, please, I understand that this painting has been in your family home for many generations. And he may even be an ancestor of yours…"

"I am not related to them at all," Lockhart said with great arrogance.

She wanted to ask questions but knew that if she spoke to him like she had on the bus, Gran would throw her out and she would never have the painting.

"And," Hannah continued, "I realise that the portrait may have some sentimental value, then. I am willing to pay for it." She had Cassidy's money. "I have three thousand Canadian dollars in my bag. It's yours for the portrait." She looked at the older woman hopefully. "That's—what?—nearly two thousand British pounds, right?"

Gran spouted off some quickly spoken lingo to Jake.

"My grandmother is worried that the portrait has" — he rolled his eyes—"bewitched you or the spirit has taken you over and is coercing you to do this. She does not want you to be hurt by it."

"He won't hurt me. He has never hurt you. He has never hurt anyone in this house. You can't even see him."

"Tell her I am here right now."

"He is here right now."

Gran made the sign of the cross again.

Jake's eyes shifted side to side. "You can see it?"

"He's not an 'it'," Hannah defended. "Wouldn't you like him out of your house? If I take the painting, he will no longer be here. It is the portrait that keeps him trapped here. And even if I can't return him to where he came from, I will not return him here to you. I will take him home with me."

"You will?" Lockhart asked, his head snapping around to look at her.

"Yes, I will," she promised, looking into his eyes as the two people in the room looked at her oddly. "Please, may I take him? The painting?"

Gran spoke rapidly again.

"You know that she understands everything you are saying, and she can probably speak it if she can understand it," Lockhart drawled.

Hannah nodded again, surreptitiously.

"Ah, Gran," Jake said, shaking his head at the old woman. "She says you can take it but she wants the money." Jake didn't sound like he agreed, but maybe it would pay for school for Jake and that made Hannah happy.

Hannah let out a little whoop. She rooted in her bag and handed Gran the money.

"Jake, you wanna help me take the portrait down?"

"Sure," he answered slowly. "How are you going to move it, or ship it?"

"Mmm, we hadn't thought that far. Shall I rent a van?" she asked Lockhart.

"I think that would be best," he answered.

"How long will it take to drive there?"

"I don't know. I have never driven in a motor car until today on the...bus." He said the word slowly as if he'd never before pronounced the word. "We had horses in my time."

"Right," Hannah breathed.

Jake looked at her, blinking. "Are you really talking to it, er, him?"

She nodded.

Jake shook his head and tromped up the stairs.

With some hard work and some strategy, Hannah and Jake were able to take the portrait from the wall and lay it down on the floor, no thanks to Lockhart, who barked orders the whole time.

"Now what?" Jake asked.

"Well, I guess I'll go rent a van and I'll need some kind of packaging to wrap him in so that he doesn't get damaged."

"I've got a bunch of cardboard in the barn—you're welcome to that. I was just going to burn it."

Hannah looked at Lockhart. "Will that be enough? Will that keep it safe? I mean, what will happen if you get damaged in any way? What if I accidentally put a hole in you? Will it hurt you, or worse?"

"I think I'm dead, Hannah, how much worse can it get?"

"Famous last words, Lock."

He smiled and her heart skipped a beat.

"What are you smiling at?" she asked.

"You referred to me as Lock. I have not been addressed as such since childhood."

She smiled warmly at him.

"Okay, stop, you guys are freakin' me out," Jake interrupted. "All this one-sided conversation is just crackers."

"Okay, I'm going to rent a van." Hannah started for the stairway. Jake hammered down the stairs behind her, obviously not comfortable staying with the painting.

"I'm coming with you," Jake announced.

Hannah rented a van equipped with GPS. It would take six hours and fifty-eight minutes to drive to Airdrie, Scotland—approximately six hundred sixty-three kilometres. She found out it was not that far from Glasgow, and with a little more research, she found that Trafalis Hall indeed still existed after all this time.

Jake packed up the portrait, helped her load it, gave her a quick lesson on right-hand driving, and waved goodbye as she and Lockhart pulled out of the drive.

Chapter Eight

Hannah and Lockhart crossed the border into Scotland. She could see that he grew more anxious the further they drove.

"How do you feel?" she asked. "A few more hours and you will be home."

"I am anxious to see my home, but I feel strangely sad knowing that my family will no longer be there. They are long past."

"I'm sorry."

"Do not be."

"Are you sure that your descendants will know what to do to free you?" she asked sceptically.

"There are secrets within the painting. They will know what to do."

"But things get lost and forgotten through time, Lock. What if they don't know? What if they won't even see me when we get there?" Hannah almost hoped they wouldn't. She wasn't ready to let him go. She didn't want to think about leaving him and going home without him. Hannah knew rationally that they could never have a real relationship but she couldn't seem to bear the thought of never seeing him again. She'd grown so attached to him in so little time—it scared her.

"Then I will hang for eternity in the great hall of your dwelling in your beloved Can-a-dia," he said, turning warm, dark eyes on her.

"It's Canada," she whispered, correcting him.

"You say we will reach Airdrie within hours?" he asked.

She nodded.

"You must stop to rest." The desire in his eyes warmed her.

Hannah looked over at Lockhart quickly, needing to keep her eyes on the road—driving on the wrong side of the road, let alone the wrong side of the vehicle, took some serious concentration. But she was elated that not only did he want to prolong their time together, he wanted to spend it making love to her.

"If I check into a hotel, will you be able to stay out of the painting for any length of time if it is a fair distance from you? I mean, we'll be in the room and the portrait will be in the van in the parking lot."

"I'm not sure how long I will be able to stay with you, but I will try. Perhaps I should go back in now so that I may have more time later?"

Hannah shrugged.

"Protect yourself, Hannah," he said, preparing her for the dizziness that would precede and follow his vanishing.

Hannah drove another half hour or so then checked into a hotel and ordered room service. While she waited for Lockhart, she had a shower and slipped into a pretty, delicate pink, bustle-backed nightie that she'd purchased, complete with barely-there matching panties. She looked into the mirror, making sure the tight fitting bodice tucked nicely under her breasts, showing the swell and side slope, perfectly revealing her shape.

Hannah held onto the sink as light-headedness overcame her.

"You could not be lovelier," Lockhart's deep voice sounded from behind her. She looked into the mirror as he skimmed his hand across her shoulder. He ran his hands all over her. "Clothing in your time is made to tempt and tease a man, yeah?" His lips grazed her skin, making her shiver.

"And not in your time? Corsets and ladies' décolletage were not tempting to you?"

He reached around her, easing his warm fingers into her panties, cupping her soft smooth mound. He nuzzled her ear as he whispered, "A man would kill for this."

"You *are* fascinated by that, aren't you?" She smiled, pleased by his reaction. She pulled his hand out, making him wait.

"It makes me think of nothing else. I want to dive between your legs every time I see you." He squeezed her again, his finger fitting neatly between her lips, pushing the fabric against her clit, creating delicious friction. "I want to take it with me. Put it in my pocket."

She giggled at the ridiculous notion until he continued, "Then I could touch you and play with you, stroke you with my fingers. And when that wasn't enough, I could take it out and kiss you, lick you, plunge my tongue deep inside you. I could walk around for eternity with the taste of you in my mouth."

Hannah turned into his arms. "You say all the right things," she said, then engaged him in a deep, rousing kiss. She backed him towards the bed, unlacing his breeches as she did. When the back of his knees hit the bed, she knelt in front of him. His eyes warmed when he realised what she wanted to do to him. She yanked at the tight-fitting material, removing it. She took his cock in her hand, stroking the length of him, pulling the extra skin at the head taut. She licked around it, teasing, tasting. He moaned, sweeping his hands into her hair.

Hannah looked up and pointed at him. "If you lose control and grab the back of my head and make me choke, I will never do this for you again," she warned, trying not to think that she might never see him again.

Lockhart eased his hands back, palms up in surrender, the tension she was creating in him etched in the hard line of his jaw, the slight wrinkling around his eyes.

"That's better." She smiled, licking her lips before taking the head of his jerking cock into her mouth once more. She made sure to let her saliva run until it was dripping through her fingers, making the slide slick and nicely lubricated.

He moaned loudly. "Your mouth is so hot."

Hannah stroked one hand down his shaft, holding him while her other palm held his balls firmly. Lock inhaled sharply. She eased her mouth down over his hot, distended penis one slow inch at a time, then back up to the tip, going just a little farther with every glide, increasing the pressure with her lips on the ascent.

He shifted, widening his stance, trying to support his weakening knees.

When she reached the limit that her throat could take, Hannah picked up the pace, synchronising her mouth and the hand that she had wrapped around the thick base. She felt the surging rush of his excitement bubbling just under the surface of his taut skin.

He tried to elbow her away before he ejaculated. She laid a comforting hand on his stomach. She released him briefly from the hot confines of her jaw. "No, let me do this," she soothed, letting him know that it was all right for her to do so, knowing things might have been different in his time.

She continued the tempo he liked until he came in her mouth. His hips relaxed forward as his tension eased. He slid his fingers into her hair, stroking her tenderly. She swallowed, licking every last drop from the tip before she released him.

Lockhart pulled her into his arms and laid her on the bed gently as if she were made of glass. He eased down beside her and hugged her tightly, kissing her cheeks. He cupped her cheek softly.

Hannah looked up into his dark eyes and the air rushed from her lungs. His gaze was so soft—almost loving, she thought.

"No one has ever done that for me," he confessed and Hannah's satisfaction soared. "Why would you want to?"

"You enjoy the taste of me. You said so. So why would I not also want the taste of you in my mouth...for all eternity?" she said, almost as an afterthought, but was somewhat surprised to find she meant it.

His brow furrowed. "You would...want that?" he questioned slowly, his eyes searching hers. "Eternity, with me?"

She didn't answer—it was a moot question. He was a painting. But if he were real, she would.

"How is it…that can happen?" she asked, confused. "I mean, how is that you have human functions, cravings and reactions if you are a ghost?"

"I don't know. I don't know how it all works. I'm not even sure that I am a ghost."

Hannah bit her lip asking another question that was plaguing her. "How did it happen? How did you get trapped in the painting?"

He took a deep breath. "My father commissioned an artist, a MacAllister, to paint my portrait for the family gallery. It is tradition in my family. We were surprised when the artist arrived and it was a woman. Her name was Lillias. Women did not do such things then. Of course, the scope of the project made it imperative that I make myself available to pose, and Lillias had to stay in residence at Trafalis. We spent vast amounts of time together."

Hannah knew where this was going. Lockhart was a very handsome, charismatic man. It was difficult not to fall in love with him. "You fell in love."

"Well, I had a dalliance, a brief flirtation. She, on the other hand, read more into it than I was willing to give."

"You used her?"

"No, I did not. I did not make promises, and I did not take her innocence. I simply made the time that I was subjected to a little more *bearable* for myself."

"But you seduced her into intimate things that might lead a woman, especially in your time, to believe that you made promises?"

He looked away. "Perhaps. I was mischievous, even then. I did not realise how much I had hurt her until it was too late. She was incensed. She said I had promised to marry her. But I was leaving to fulfil my duties as a soldier—I had no need or desire for a wife.

My life was only just beginning. On my last night home, she lured me with food and wine, said she would unveil the portrait, that it was finally finished. I drank the wine and I knew immediately that she'd laced it with some poison. My body became immoveable. I could see and hear, but I could not move or speak."

Hannah listened intently.

"Lillias ushered a woman, dressed in long flowing dark robes, into my chamber and they lit awful-smelling herbs and chanted in strange tongues. And I began to feel not myself. I felt as if I were floating. It was like everything that made me corporeal began to break apart."

"That's how I feel every time you appear," Hannah exclaimed.

He nodded his understanding, continuing, "Piece by piece my body shifted and reassembled inside the painting. At first I stood, just as you see the portrait now, unaware that I could move, but I could see."

"That's how you saw me," Hannah said. "You weren't being a voyeur at all. You were watching through the eyes of the painting. That's how you knew that I wanted to kiss you."

"Yes. Do you know what that did you me, lass, to see the desire for me in your eyes? I wanted you to kiss me. I wanted to kiss you. That's why when you came upon me, I could not resist. Not you or the need."

"So that woman in the dark robes, she was some kind of witch or sorceress?"

"Aye. She cursed me into the painting and Lillias taunted me with her words and she tempted me with her body. She said that if I would only give my love to her, I could be free. But I was angry. The last thing I would ever do was love the woman who had sentenced me to this hell. But she could not understand why her plan had not worked. She summoned the witch and as I remember it explained, in the way the spell was worded I did not have to give my love to Lillias for the spell to be broken as was her wish. The witch took it upon herself to teach us both a lesson. To teach me not to be so uncaring of others' emotions or so selfish, and Lillias needed to learn that you cannot force someone to love you when they do not. When Lillias realised that I would never return her love, she jumped from my chamber window. I watched it happen. There was nothing I could do."

"Have you learned your lesson?"

"Aye. Time is a relentless teacher."

"Then why is the spell not broken?"

"I don't know. Perhaps it is because Lillias did not live to learn hers? Perhaps our destinies were tied? I do not know how it all works, Hannah. I am still learnin'. These things that have happened between us these past days are all new to me. Before you, I had given up hope. I would spend eternity, roaming, alone. But since I met you, I feel differently, like you and home are the keys to my freedom."

"How is it you ended up in Wales?"

"The witch, I came to find, was also a MacAllister and her guilt over Lillias' death was more than she could bear. She held me solely responsible for it all and vowed that if Lillias would never find happiness then I would not either. She had me stolen from the gallery and sent to Wales. This is why I believe that I must return home. But it was in Wales that I discovered that I could remove myself from the painting. It was not something that I could do at home, not even in anger."

"Did you not miss your home terribly?"

"Of course. I miss my family. When I disappeared Lillias told me in one of her nastier moments that everyone believed that I had deserted, that I was a coward. But my father never believed it. He knew how eager I was to serve. He came and he spoke to me, in the painting, after Lillias killed herself but before I was stolen. He didn't even know that I was bound to it, but he knew that some mishap had befallen me and he vowed to find out what had happened. But he and the rest of my family are long since past. Trafalis is all that remains. It is the only thing that remembers me. The only thing I am bound to, besides the portrait."

"You said it was anger that made you realise that you could step from the painting, and it was anger that also allowed you to leave Jake's house to come after me on the bus."

"Aye."

"So, perhaps strong emotion will also help break the curse?"

"I am feeling strong emotion right now, Hannah-lass," he said rotating his hips into her. "Shall we see if you taught me well how to please you?" His dark eyes warmed as he positioned himself over her. He skimmed his closed lips over the swell of her breasts still hidden under soft pink silk.

He pressed his warm lips to her nipple. She felt his hot, moist breath through the material. He circled her softly as she felt his finger round the other side. She smiled as she remembered doing the same to him. He followed her instructions admirably. But as his own excitement grew, the aggressive, unschooled roughness that was so undeniably a part of him took over, and Hannah quickly realised she liked it very much. His touch was less bruising but still heavy-handed. He pulled on the delicate bodice, exposing her heated skin. She both felt and heard the material rip.

"You are depleting my wardrobe rapidly." She chuckled.

"I'm sorry," he breathed heavily before he wrapped his hot lips around the stiff peak. He laved and stroked the tight buds, plucking with his fingers while flicking with his rough tongue, stoking her insides until she was writhing beneath him. It felt like an invisible tether spanned from her burning nipples straight to the core of her, making her wet, hot centre clench and release with anticipation of him sinking his hot cock into her. Hannah arched, trying to get closer to him, her breasts straining for more. Her heart pounded, her mouth went dry, a fine sheen of sweat beaded her skin as he re-educated her as to what she liked.

There was nothing artificial about Lockhart. He hadn't picked up any bad habits or retold the same lines in the newest chick-flick to try to seduce her, like every other guy she'd been with. He hadn't been tainted by Hollywood or porn. She would never hear him say *you complete me*, or *God, baby, can you fuck*. He did what he wanted — if something felt good to him, he did it. There was nothing choreographed or copied. Even his dialogue was natural and spontaneous. She knew when he enjoyed something by the sounds that came out of his perfect mouth, and she found she liked to hear it. He didn't hold back. If he wanted to growl at her like an animal, he did so. He was completely genuine. He was the real deal.

Replacing his tongue with his fingers, still stimulating both breasts, he kissed his way down her body, tonguing the hollow column between her ribs, circling her belly button. She squirmed under him, whimpering with need, pushing her panties out of the way for him. The fine stubble on his chin grazed her bare skin, heightening her arousal. He ran his smooth lips over the bare skin hooding her aching clit, making her blood boil.

"By the Christ, Hannah, I canna get enough of this."

She wanted him to lick her so bad that she lifted her hips off the bed, presenting the burning nub to his hot, probing tongue. He stopped teasing her breasts, caressing firmly down her ribs before he pushed her panties down her legs and off her ankles.

"Ahh!" she cried out in ecstasy, bunching her hands into the sheets in frustration. He squared her with his hands, using his thumbs to spread her lips back from the pulsing bud, exposing the sensitive tissue to first the cold air, then his hot breath. He expelled a deep moan of appreciation, only heightening her need to feel his tongue in her. She cried out as he sucked her clit into his mouth, circling his pointed tongue and grazing the responsive centre as wave after wave of pounding pleasure sent her hips into a rolling frenzy.

Hannah pulled Lockhart by the hair, tugging his mouth away from her greedy cunt. "Fuck me now!" she demanded through her teeth.

His head angled to the side, and she realised belatedly that women probably didn't speak like that in his time, but her demanding hips and body brought him around to understanding in a hurry. Lock knelt in front of her as she contorted, trying to grasp his thick shaft, butting the head of his penis against her contracting pussy and pushing her knees back, placing her feet on his hips. He inched into her as she stretched to accommodate him. She shimmied her hips, wanting to feel all of him deep inside.

Lockhart caressed from her ankle, slowly over her calves, skimming her quivering thighs. "You have no hair anywhere," he marvelled again. "Even your legs are smooth as silk." He captured her hips forcefully and thrust himself deeply into her.

"Oh, God. Yes!" She tucked her hands behind her knees and pulled them back even farther as he pumped his hips vigorously, increasing the delectable pressure that was building inside her. Hannah began to climax almost immediately, the velvet slide of his substantial rod sending her into a spasming whirl of pleasure. "Oh, God, Lock, you feel so good!" she whimpered as he continued to pound into her, his heavy balls slapping against her ass, until he finally bellowed his release.

Lockhart eased down beside her, making sure to keep them connected. Hannah was still so stimulated that her pussy kept clenching and undulating at his every breath — every jerk or movement of his deflating erection sent little pulses of deep satisfying pleasure to some dark place deep inside her.

"Mmm." Lock's chest rumbled at one such clench around him. He smoothed Hannah's hair from her face and he looked softly into her eyes. "If only I could cast my own curse. I would make time stand still and we would spend eternity just like this."

The look in his dark eyes held some emotion that she could not bring herself to name, afraid what they were feeling was merely the gratification that came with the afterglow of good loving. Hannah swallowed thickly as her eyes searched his. She bit her lip and grazed her fingertip through the small dent in his sculpted chin.

"Just think—I had to cross an ocean to find a man like you."

"And I had to cross time to find you. I love you, Hannah-lass."

Hannah's lips parted on a gasp of surprise just as she felt the room shift and weave. Nausea slammed into her as Lockhart was whisked away from her, but not before she saw the sorrow and finality in his dark eyes.

"Oh, no!" She scrambled up out of the bed. "No...no!" she cried, afraid this time was different, that he would never leave the portrait again after his declaration. Had they broken the curse? Had she just lost him forever?

She carelessly pulled on a T-shirt and shorts, and, grabbing the keys to the rent-a-van, she tore off to the parking lot. She unlocked the back double doors and leapt into the back of the truck. "Lock, oh please, Lockhart, don't leave me."

Hannah tore at the brown postage paper that Jake had covered the portrait with. She uncovered Lockhart's handsome face and she knew immediately that it had changed. The portrait had always been convincingly life-like to her, but now it was flat and unnatural. He was no longer there. He was gone. They'd broken the curse.

"No," she whimpered, barely feeling the hot tears that ran down her cheeks. "Not yet. Why?" She asked the still visage for answers. "Why did you say it? We didn't have enough time!" she wailed, knowing in her heart that any amount of time with him would never have been enough. She lay down on top of the painting, her head on his chest, crying his name over and over.

Finally, she pushed the packing paper back over his face. Hannah slammed the van door. She stumbled blindly through her tears back to the room, threw herself on the bed, and stared unseeingly at the ceiling.

Chapter Nine

The next morning, Hannah got into the rental van and continued the trip to Trafalis Hall in Airdrie, alone. She would return Lockhart to his home, as she'd promised. That was where he wanted to be, that was where she would leave him. Home.

It was a lovely day. Beautiful sunlight lit the amazing countryside, but Hannah didn't enjoy any of it, angry that the sun would shine at all when her grief was so raw. She remembered this feeling all too well.

She half-expected Lockhart to pop up in the seat next to her, just as she'd prayed last night that he would come to her when he was able. But she knew in her heart that he was gone. He would never appear to her again. Tears ran unchecked down her cheeks as she drove. She followed the GPS's directions, finding that Trafalis Hall was a museum complete with the blue and gold plaque designating it as a historical site.

"Oh, Lock, your home is famous," she whispered as she drove up the long, winding drive. He would get a kick out of that, she thought. A man as arrogant as he was would take pleasure in knowing that his legacy had lived on in some way. She wished she could tell him. She hoped that, wherever he was, he knew.

Hannah parked the van and stepped out so that she could get a good look at the Hall that Lock had grown up in and loved so much. She gaped at the enormous stone castle. She'd seen this place before. The night that she'd driven up the driveway of Jake and Gran's in Wales, the lightning had flashed and she'd seen this very castle, but driving from it the next day, it had been an old farmhouse. Hannah shivered.

She walked up the wending stone walkway, expecting to have to pay for a ticket to get in, but there was no one around. The place seemed to be deserted. She pushed open the heavy, ornate door.

"Hello?" Her voice seemed to carry. She listened. Way off in the distance she could hear hammering, like someone was repairing or building something.

She looked down the four long corridors, all lined with massive portraits cordoned off with velvet ropes. Rich-looking red runners ran the length of each hallway housing the ancestors and descendents of the Munro clan through the centuries.

"Hello?" she tried again. The hammering stopped. "Hello, is anyone here?"

She heard footsteps nearing her.

"Can I help ya?" a deep Scottish brogue purred from behind her — scaring the daylights out of her.

"Oh, I, uh…" She turned to match the face with the voice and she began to tremble. "Lock?" she whispered, staring at a man who looked very much like Lockhart — the same thick, dark hair but cut short, worn in a contemporary male style. He was wearing a T-shirt that hugged his muscular chest and showed off his biceps nicely. A pair of snug, ripped jeans slung low on his hips. He looked amazing in modern clothing.

"Lock?" she said, again.

"Aye, lass, I'm Llach. Llachlan Munro, can I help ya?"

It was Lockhart, but it wasn't. He looked just like him but he didn't recognise her. Hannah felt that intense deep grief constrict in her chest as she watched the deep chocolate eyes assessing her raw, tear-streaked cheeks.

Hannah closed her eyes and swallowed convulsively. "Llachlan Munro," she repeated, trying to shake the cobwebs from her brain. This was not Lock.

"Are ya lookin' for someone?" he asked in a familiar deep brogue. He watched her closely with dark familiar eyes.

"Lockhart Munro," she whispered, trembling violently as dark edges formed a tunnel around her vision.

"Lockhart Munro?" the man said, sending another shudder through Hannah's weak form as Lock's name passed his lips. "Lockhart Munro has been missin' from these halls for hundreds of years, lass."

"I found him. I've brought him home." She sniffed as fresh tears formed in her eyes.

His eyes widened. "You did, did you?" His perfect mouth formed a devastating smile, drawing Hannah's eye to the slight cleft in his perfectly formed chin, complete with a dusting of uneven stubble.

"Yes, I have the portrait in a van out front."

"Let's have a look, then," he said, rubbing his hands together eagerly.

He followed Hannah out into the sunshine. She opened the doors of the van and he jumped agilely inside. She didn't feel the need to follow him and look into Lockhart's beautiful face again. It hurt too much.

He pulled the torn paper aside. "Is this some kinda joke then, lass?" he asked, looking back at her.

"Excuse me?"

"It is an exquisite antique frame and it is even in the style of all the other portraits that adorn Trafalis Hall, but where is the portrait?"

"What do you mean where is the portrait? It's inside the frame."

He lifted a perfect dark brow. "You call this a portrait? It's all but ruined, lass."

Hannah stepped inside and looked down. The canvas was all peeled and tattered as if it had been left out in the rain. Her tears could not have done that, she reasoned quickly. Lockhart's beautiful face was all but obscured, as if the paint had aged and weathered over the last four hundred years, only overnight. Her mouth opened in shock. "But…it… I… This is not how I found it."

He looked up at her from his squatted position. "Here, help me get it inside and we'll have a good look. Perhaps it can be restored, if the deterioration is not too bad. We've had some luck restoring some of the others."

Llachlan and Hannah carefully manoeuvred the painting inside. They laid it on the floor in the massive foyer and Llachlan pulled off the packing material.

"Mmm, it's pretty bad, miss. Where did ya find it?"

"In Wales."

"In Wales? How on earth would it have ended up in Wales?" He walked around it, not waiting for her to answer. "How did ya know to bring it here?"

She didn't know how to answer that. "Do you know anything about the painting or about Lockhart Munro?"

"Aye, it's quite a legend around here." His eyes danced with amusement. "There's even a space allocated on the wall of Lockhart's wing for the portrait. Would ya like to see it?"

Lockhart's wing? "Yes. I would."

He grinned, seemingly only too happy to share his family's history with her.

They passed modern-looking portraits, painted in the style of Lockhart's time but with contemporary materials. "That's you," Hannah remarked as they passed the one of Llachlan. He leaned on a polo mallet instead of a sword.

He smiled crookedly. "Aye, 'tis family tradition to pose."

"Is it family tradition to have a MacAllister paint the portraits?"

"Oh, so you know some of the legend, too. No. MacAllisters are banned from Trafalis Hall," he said, but she wasn't sure if he was joking or not.

"Good," Hannah responded, thinking the whole line should be banished to hell. She looked to the next portrait. Another man with fairer hair and complexion but with a similar look to Lockhart and Llachlan sat atop a dark horse. "That is my brother, Malcolm. As you can see, I am the better-lookin' of the two." He grinned cockily, bringing out a dimple in his left cheek. Even his teasing arrogance reminded her of Lock.

"And so full of humility, too, I see."

Llachlan chuckled as he moved to the next. "That one is the wedding portrait of our parents. Kerr and Muirial."

"You are a lovely family," Hannah said wistfully, running her fingers covetously over the swirls of paint that made up the lacy hem of his mother's wedding gown. She suddenly felt very empty and alone.

"Thank you," he said in a deep voice. "Come see the ancient ones."

The ancient ones, she thought. Lockhart wasn't ancient to her.

"Lockhart and his parents are down this corridor." He walked slowly, leading Hannah. He stopped in front of an older gentleman dressed elaborately. "Lockhart's father was also named Llachlan—I am named after him," he informed her. She looked up and would have known this was Lockhart's father without being told. He was just an older version of the man she'd known. She ran an affectionate hand over his name.

"And this is Lockhart's mum, Eveolyn," Llachlan continued. Hannah looked up at the woman's face. She was stunning, but what else was to be expected when her son was so devastatingly handsome?

Llachlan stepped to the next portrait, saying nothing. Hannah looked up to see Lockhart. She wavered and Llachlan's strong arms came around her.

"But...how...?" she questioned. "It looks exactly like the portrait I brought..." The words died away as she realised it wasn't the same at all. There was writing on the bottom of this painting.

"As the legend goes, the original Llachlan Munro, Lockhart's father, had another portrait done exactly as the original that Lillias MacAllister painted. He never believed that his son would evade his duty."

"He didn't," Hannah defended, turning in his arms. He watched her steadily.

"As his father held to until the day he died and even beyond. You will read the inscription."

"'*Selfishness has sealed your fate,*
Within this frame your punishment take,
Obsessive love now torn asunder,
Love's pure heart will find another.'"

She read it then looked at him, confused.

"It is the spell the MacAllister witch cursed him with."

"Ohhh." Hannah's eyes filled again as her breath rushed from her lungs at the thought that she'd just repeated the dreaded words that had bound him to the painting. "How do you know this?"

"As I said, Lockhart's father never gave up on him or the hope that they would find the keys that would unlock his son. It took him many years but he finally found the witch and she armed him with everything he needed to break the curse, including the spell. Everything, that is, except the whereabouts of the painting. His father documented everything and it has been passed down from generation to generation ever since."

Llachlan moved them along to the next frame. It was another painting of Lockhart, as he might have looked if he'd grown any older. "His father commissioned another portrait, perhaps in his declining years, having the artist age his ageless son for him."

Hannah looked up at him with tears in her eyes. "Ahh, he would have still been so handsome." Hannah read the next epitaph without thinking.

"'*Within this frame, your curse is time,*
Learn your lessons, learn the rhyme,
Time will flee until you find,
The heart and soul not of this time.'"

Was she the heart and soul not of this time? Had she been his key to freedom as he had hoped? How could she ever be sure that he was free and happy wherever he went? Warm tears coursed down her cheeks.

"You seem very moved by the painting, lass. Almost as if it were real to you. It was speculated in the documents that I have read... It was believed Lockhart could move outside of the painting. Is it true? Have you seen him, lass?"

"Yes," she admitted, no longer caring if he would think her crazy. The warm empathy in his eyes undid her.

"I am not one to baulk at things that I do not understand. I've seen things in this very hall that I cannot explain. But if you have broken the curse for Lockhart, by returning him home, then allow yourself to feel relief for him that he is in a better place. He should have been dead for at least three hundred and fifty years, lass. You've freed his soul to find its rightful resting place. He is finally at peace. Take solace in that."

But now would she ever find peace? "May I have a moment," she gulped, not wanting to hear his words. To her, Lockhart had been very much alive only a few hours ago. And he'd never been given the chance to live his life. It was so unfair.

He bowed formally. "Of course." She watched him walk away.

Hannah placed her back against the wall and slid down it dejectedly. "Why didn't you tell me that you would never come out again? Or did you and I was too stupid to understand the consequences?" She sighed. "And here we are—in your home, just as you wanted, and your descendents are here. What happened to '*There are secrets in the painting, lass, they'll know what to do'*? You knew that just bringing you back would set you free." She slammed her elbow against the wall in anger. "I would have stayed with you, you know. I meant it when I said that if I met a man like you that I would stay. I would have made it work somehow even if we'd only been given whatever time you were allowed to be free of the painting. It would have been enough." She wiped her face.

"But maybe Llachlan is right. After so many years of desolation and loneliness, freedom is your reward. And I should not be selfish for I will only have to endure one lifetime without you."

She didn't know how long she sat there before Llachlan stood over her. "Come, English, there will be no more cryin'." He held a hand down to her.

She looked at him, shaking her head slightly, remembering Lockhart calling her 'English'. "It's Hannah. Hannah Keys," she said, placing her hand in his and allowing him to pull her to her feet.

He grinned. "How appropriate, Miss Keys."

She blinked, swaying forward into his arms, feeling quite dizzy, the tunnel vision returning. "He looked just like you," she whispered, touching his cheek. Llachlan held that same pulling magnetism that Lockhart had.

"So I've been told," he said, setting her on her feet. He stroked her wet cheek. He backed her against the portrait, his eyes on her lips, as if he might kiss her. "I feel like I know ya, lass…"

"You do," she whispered. "I love you, too."

He took her hand in his. "'*Heart in home, hand in hand*
The keys come from another land
To free me from this hell on earth
Love's own tear shall break the curse.'"

He wiped his thumb across her cheek as a gust of wind blew up around them. Hannah shrieked as they tumbled backward into a vortex of sound and light.

"Oh shit! Not now!" Llachlan cursed. "Hold on!" She felt his strong arms around her as wind whipped around them. She tucked her head under his chin and locked her hands around his strong back. She closed her eyes tight to the blinding light. She couldn't hear. The pressure in her head made it feel like it was going to pop, that her ears would bleed. Just when she thought that she couldn't endure another minute they were thrown to the ground. The wind and sound died away. Hannah struggled to catch her breath.

Chapter Ten

Hannah opened her eyes slowly, swallowing convulsively, trying not to throw up. She was no longer in the portrait gallery. She sat up slowly. She looked to be in a bedroom. There were candles all around. A roaring fire in the stone fireplace. The acrid smell of incense or some other herbal aromatic permeated the air, sticking in her throat.

"Llachlan?" She realised he was no longer wrapped around her. "Llachlan?" She felt panic slither through her chest.

She stood, almost tripping over herself. She looked down to find herself dressed in an elaborate soft pink gown. "What the hell?" Her hand flew to her mouth as she realised she spoke with a Scottish burr.

She pulled the huge skirt up and she ran to the door, flinging it open. "Llach—" she started to yell but ran squarely into a solid chest.

"Aye, lass," he said, his strong arms coming around her.

"Oh, thank God! What the hell happened?"

"I'd be watchin' your mouth, lassie, or your da will give ya the switchin' of your life." His accent was incredibly thick, she thought.

She looked up slowly, her mouth opening in surprise. "Lockhart?" she breathed.

"Aye," he grinned. "Were ya expectin' someone else?"

"Ohhh!" She threw her arms around his neck, attacking his lips with hers. "Oh, God, I've missed you!"

He kissed her hard then set her away from him. "What's all this, lass? Would ya be tryin' to seduce me inta stayin'?" he said, looking into the room and closing the door. Hannah looked around the room, too. There were trays of food and wine elaborately laid out next to the massive bed that dominated the room. It certainly looked like a seduction. She gazed back at him. He was dressed differently than what he'd worn in the portrait. His tunic was similar in cut with the laces drawing the two sides together. His breeches were snug, just as she remembered. He had on the shiny black boots.

"I didn't do this," she said, not recognising her own voice or accent.

"Lillias, come now—you will stop with the game playin'. I am leavin' on the morrow and there is nuthin' you can do to change my mind."

Lillias? "I'm not Lillias. Lockhart, don't you recognise me?"

"And who would ya be bein' if ya are not Lillias MacAllister?" he asked levelling her with an intolerant look and placing his hands on his hips.

"It's me, it's Hannah," she said, pointing to her chest.

"Hannah?" He looked amused. "Hannah, ya say. Do ya think pretendin' ta be someone else will convince me to stay?" He looked down her dress where her breasts were pushed up to the absolute limit. He took his index finger and traced it over the curves, his pupils dilating as he watched. "Not only the food and wine, but you dress to tempt me. Think you I do not see what you are up to?"

He swaggered to the carafe of wine and poured himself a cup.

"I don't know what is happening to me," Hannah whispered. "I think I have lost my mind."

"I do have that effect on the lasses." He grinned again, arrogantly, bringing out the dimple in his left cheek. She looked more closely. At the moment, he reminded her more of Llachlan.

"Oh, I need to find Llachlan." She remembered what she was about.

"My father? Why on earth would you be thinkin' of him now, Lillias?"

"Your...father..." she said slowly. Right, Llachlan said that he'd been named after Lockhart's father. And Lockhart seemed to think she was Lillias. She wiped at her brow. "I...I needed to tell him that the portrait is finished," Hannah heard herself say.

"Aye, that's why I am here, is it not? You were going to *unveil* it for me?" he answered, suggestively letting his eyes travel over her décolletage.

Hannah cocked her head and looked at him steadily. He swirled the wine around the glass then toasted her with it. Lockhart's voice came to her. *On my last night home, she lured me with food and wine, said she would* unveil *the portrait, that it was finally finished. I drank the wine and I knew immediately that she'd laced it with some poison.*

The wine was almost to his lips. Hannah flew across the room, batting the offending liquid out of his hand.

"What are ya doin'? Have ya lost your mind?" He stood staring at her.

"It's very likely," she said, taking the carafe of red wine and tossing it through the chamber casement. Hannah clenched her hands into fists as another unbidden thought slammed into her. It was the oriel where Lillias threw herself to her death.

Hannah looked down from where she stood, staring at the dark red liquid staining the stone below, growing larger as it spread. She could almost picture Lillias' prone body lying below — or her own, since at the moment Lockhart seemed to see her as Lillias. Had she ever known the kind of grief and despair that could drive someone to do something so final in the heat of a moment?

There was a knock at the door. Lockhart's eyes narrowed suspiciously.

"Were ya hopin' ta trap me? Is that what this is all aboot? Have ya set us up to be caught in some kind of tryst?"

She shook her head in denial and rushed for the door. A woman dressed all in black darkened the opening. "Have ya given him the wine then, Lillias?" she whispered, placing a dark satchel into Hannah's hands.

It was the witch, Hannah guessed from Lockhart's description.

She shook her head again. "No, he has consumed no wine."

"Then I'll come back. Make sure he drinks it all."

Hannah gripped her arm. "*No*! No, I've changed my mind. I'll not do this. Do not come back." Perhaps this was her chance to free Lockhart for all time. She had never been sure that he had been released to go onto his afterlife. For all she knew, now that the portrait was returned to Trafalis Hall, he was trapped inside forever. He'd told her that when he was at the Hall he was unable to move freely. He hadn't been able to free himself from the painting until he'd found himself in Wales at Gran's. If they all believed that she was Lillias, she could prevent this from happening in the first place.

The woman recoiled. "What! You were so sure! Begged me..."

"Who is it?" Lockhart said, losing patience, pulling the door wide.

"It is just my aunt," Hannah lied as Lillias. "She will tell no one that she saw us together here."

Lockhart looked her up and down. "So was this the plan then? Ta have your *aunt* go to your father and seal my fate? Would ya seriously go ta these lengths to force me to marry ya?" He looked at her accusingly.

"No. No, I never meant for any of this to happen." Hannah thrust the satchel back into the witch's grasp. "*Go!* Just go!" she said, shooing with her hand then shutting the door on the offensive woman. She turned to Lockhart. "I never meant for this to happen. I just wanted you to see the finished portrait. Now I will go. No one need ever know that I was here alone with you." Hannah pulled open the door but he captured her by the elbow, stopping her.

He pushed the door shut and backed her against it. He looked down at her, his eyes hot and challenging. He shook his head and grinned slightly. "I knew ya couldn't go through with it. How could ya think that you were a match for me? I need a woman who is my equal. You've done nothing this whole time we've known each other but tease me. I need a woman who can meet my needs, not one who just feigns she knows what I might want. Nor do I want a woman who will lie under me unmoving. I want a woman who knows what she wants and enjoys it when she gets it. I want a partner. Not some mousy little chit—"

He didn't get to finish his sentence before she caught his shirt and pulled his mouth down to hers. She'd show him mousy! As she recalled, at first he hadn't liked that she was aggressive, but by the time she was through with him, he'd very much liked it.

She backed him towards the bed and pushed him down onto it. He pulled away and stared up at her in shock and great interest. "Lillias?"

"No. Hannah! And don't you forget it!" She thrust her hands into his hair and jerked his head back and plunged her tongue into his mouth.

He growled deep in his chest as he seized her around the waist. She could have smiled in triumph if her mouth weren't busy. She was just so happy to be back in his arms again.

He pulled her up onto the bed with him and she found herself on her back underneath him. He ground his hard cock viciously into her thigh.

"Hey, ease up. We have time."

He grunted and pulled his mouth from hers, dragging it down her neck. He was back to the untutored Lock. All male aggression and no finesse.

He clutched crudely at her breasts just as he'd done in Wales. Hannah took his hands in hers and schooled him again. His dark eyes glittered as he watched her cup and plump them. She slowly released her grip from his. But he didn't keep his hold there as she'd expected. He pulled the material of her dress down, exposing her breasts to him. He dropped his head and began nipping at the flesh and sucking too hard.

She grasped his chin firmly. "Ouch! Do you need another lesson there too, Lock?"

He cocked his head in confusion. She wiggled beneath him until her mouth was near his again. "Like this," she said pulling his lips to hers. She sucked on his lower lip softly. "Feel that?"

"Aye," he all but wheezed.

"Suck softly." She darted her tongue touching his. "Pretend your tongue is my nipple."

He groaned loudly at her words. She rotated her tongue slowly around the end of his, picking up the pace then flicking it quickly again and again.

His breathing spiked. She released him, knowing that if she continued he would explode before she got to feel his nice, hot cock inside her.

He stared at her. She directed him back to her nipple. He was overly rough at first. She stroked his cheek. "Softly, Lock. Mmm, that's it," she encouraged as he began to circle the erect bud with his tongue. She felt the exquisite wet warmth spread through her lower half. Her back arched as she tried to get closer to him.

Hannah reached down between them and greedily palmed his straining erection.

Lock bellowed loudly and surged to his knees, then clumsily fumbled with the laces of his breeches. His throbbing cock sprang free of its confines. Hannah reached for him. He elbowed her arm so that she couldn't touch him. He threw her heavy skirts out of the way, almost covering her face in his haste. She tried to push them down while he kneed her thighs open.

She felt the strange sensation of his fingers parting the hairs. *How could that be?* She had no time to think when he guided the head of his penis into her. She found it uncomfortable—almost as if she weren't stimulated enough yet to accept him. She was. Just being near Lockhart stimulated her. She was wet. She was turned on. She didn't understand.

He thrust his hips trying to push deeper into her. She found herself wanting to close her thighs as she felt the overwhelming need to keep him out.

"Relax, Lillias, 'twill only hurt for a moment," he said, grasping her hips tightly. He plunged forward.

Hannah screamed at the unexpected pain. He covered her mouth with his hand as he shuddered, finding his release.

What kind of fucked-up fate would make her endure the pain of losing her virginity twice in a lifetime, and someone else's virginity at that? As if her own miserable experience in the back of a Corolla at seventeen hadn't been enough, she'd just lost Lillias' for her. It was the experience in the back of that car that had left her less than thrilled with the prospect of future sex. She'd vowed then and there to be the one in charge of finding her own pleasure. Guys didn't seem to mind finding their own first. So why couldn't women be the same? That was why she didn't mind telling a guy what she wanted, often in explicit detail. Sometimes they kinda liked it. It was like talking dirty. And if he didn't get it, she'd show him. Like she'd done with Lock. And if he still didn't get it, he'd be down the road.

She swatted at him with both hands. "Get off me!" she screeched.

"I'm sorry. I'm sorry," he said using his weight to keep her underneath him. "I'm sorry, Lillias, I lost control. Ya so surprised me. I didn't know ya had it in ya. I didn't expect ya to be so...so..."

"Aggressive? That's what you wanted. Damn you. You won't call her mousy again, will you?"

"Her?" he asked shaking his head.

"You lied to me."

"I never lied to ya, lass."

"You said you never took her innocence," Hannah accused him.

"Her who? Who are ya talkin' aboot? Ya are'na makin' any sense." He clutched his temples. "Ya are makin' my head split. You haven't been actin' like yourself since the moment I walked in here this eve." He rolled off her and adjusted his breeches. "Who is this Hannah that you speak of?"

Hannah stood in a swirl of heavy skirts. "Perhaps now she is someone you will never meet," she retorted cryptically, hoping she'd just saved him from spending the next four hundred years wandering alone and unhappy.

She felt dizzy and nauseous. She knew what was coming next. The wind whipped her hair and skirts. Flashing light blinded her. She felt strong arms come around her once again as he lunged for her. "Llachlan!" she shouted, gripping her hands together behind his back. She tucked herself into his chest as pressure squeezed inside her skull.

Her body slammed against the hard stones of the castle floor as if she'd been dropped from a great height. It knocked the air from her, stealing her breath. Her head was the last thing to touch anything solid. It bounced viciously off the granite like a basketball. Her skull exploded with pain.

Chapter Eleven

Hannah awoke slowly to the murmur of low voices in her splitting head. She reached beside her for Lockhart but her hand fell off the bed. She opened her eyes, the light hurting. She looked to her side. She was in a single bed, very much alone. "Lock?" she croaked, trying to sit up.

"Oh, Hannah. Thank God you're awake," Cassie said, rushing forward.

"Cass? Cassie? What are you doing here?"

"What am I doing here? I was the emergency contact on your passport. They called me when you were found."

"When I was found?" Hannah raised her hand slowly to her throbbing forehead and tried to grasp onto any one thought that was hurtling through her splitting skull. "What are you talking about? Where's Lock?"

Cassie wiped a tear from her cheek and grasped Hannah's hand, her brow furrowed in concern. "Let me just ring for a nurse and I'll tell you what I know."

"Why am I in the hospital?"

Cassie tugged the bedside bell pull. "Paul, will you go find someone?" Cassie said over her shoulder.

Hannah cracked an eye to see Paul approaching the bed, his face a pale mask. He cupped Cassie's shoulder in support and patted Hannah's foot covered under the hospital blanket. "Good to see you, Hannah. Cass has been so worried about you. We both have," he said, then left to find a nurse.

Cassie perched on the side of the bed and smoothed Hannah's hair back. Hannah relaxed a little, laying her head back against the pillow.

"Cassie, where's Lock? Is he here? Have you seen him?" Hannah saw the concern on her friend's anxious face. "Is he hurt?"

"I don't know," she said slowly. "Is that someone you met in London?"

"No, I met him…" She paused, not able to remember where she'd met him. The pain throbbing in her head making it impossible to think clearly. It was like a heavy fog pressing down on her. She blinked rapidly, but it hurt. "I think I met him in Wales?" she questioned.

"I don't think you did, sweetie." Cassie wiped a tear from Hannah's cheek, a tear she'd been unaware she'd even shed.

"I didn't? What happened? Why am I here?"

"Hannie," Cassie said, rubbing her arm. "You were mugged."

"Mugged?" Hannah hiccupped. "I wasn't mugged."

Cassie nodded. "I'm sorry, sweetie, you were. They roughed you up pretty good."

Hannah shook her head, then regretted it.

"You got off the bus in Wales — alone, thanks to me. This is all my fault for letting you come here alone. The bus station was closed and you were stranded.

There was a bar down the street. The authorities think that maybe you went in there to call a cab and then when you went outside to wait, you were attacked outside the pub. God only knows what would have happened to you if that kid and his grandma didn't stop to help."

"Jake?"

"Yes, Jake. Do you remember Jake, Hannie?"

"Yes, he and his gran picked me up. The bus I got off was the last one until the next morning and they took pity on me and took me home with them to their farm. That's where I met...Lock... Cassie, why can't I remember how I met Lock?"

"It's okay, Hannah, you're just confused. The doctor said it might take a while for you to feel like yourself again. You've been out for days."

"Out? For days?"

"Yes..."

"No, that can't be. What day is it?"

"It's Monday. You've been here in the hospital since Saturday when Jake found you outside the pub."

"No. If I've been out for days, it must be like Thursday or Friday. This is my second week here, right?"

"No. You've only been gone for a little over a week. And Hannah, I've been to Jake's place to pick up your luggage. He lives in a small flat with his grandmother. They don't live on a farm."

"Yes. The farm. It looks like a" — Hannah deflated — "castle..." she finished softly, realising what she was saying. A farm that looked like a castle?

The nurse came into the room and checked Hannah over, looking into her eyes and taking her blood pressure.

"She's very confused," Cassie said with concern.

"Head injuries are a strange thing."

"Head injury?" Hannah squeaked.

"It'll come back or it won't," the nurse continued as if Hannah hadn't spoken. "But more likely than not, it will just remain lost time. It will be like her time just stopped."

"Lost time?" *It will be like her time just stopped.* The words resonated through Hannah's confused mind. She pictured Lockhart wrapped around her in bed. *'I would make time stand still and we would spend eternity just like this.'*

She had to go. She had to find him. "When can I go?" she asked the nurse suddenly.

"The doctor will be in soon. We'll need another whole series of tests and x-rays just to make sure your confusion isn't something more serious."

"I have to go."

"What's the hurry, Hannah? Let's get you well enough to travel and then we'll get you home."

"Home? I don't want to go home. I have to get back to Scotland..."

Cassie grasped her shoulders firmly. "Hannah!" she all but yelled. "You never made it to Scotland!"

"But I did. I rented the van and we took...we took... I don't remember but we were transporting something...to..."

"Listen. Remember what we planned. A week in each place? You did London for the week. You barely set foot in Wales...and that is where your trip ended. You were attacked. You never set foot in Scotland."

"No. You're wrong. I met Lock. We went Scotland... He's...there...waiting... I need to see him. Cassie?" She looked up at her friend, pleading. "I promised him I wouldn't leave."

Cassie hugged her tightly.

* * * *

Days later, Hannah was released from the hospital. The longer she was away from Lock, the more confused she became. And Cassie tried to convince her it had all been a dream or hallucination caused by the head trauma.

Cassie and Paul took her back to Swansea, where they had a room. They spoke softly to one another but Hannah still overheard their conversation.

"I'm worried, Paul. She's so quiet. She's still so confused."

Paul wound a reassuring arm around Cass. "She'll be better once we get her home, babe. You'll see."

"I hope so."

"She's been better since the physician prescribed those pills though, don't you think?"

"Yeah, I guess, she doesn't speak of that *Lock* as much on them."

"Why don't you show her the emails and the pictures that she sent you? Maybe that will help move things along for her. Maybe clear things up for her a little. Remind her of what's real and what she imagined or dreamed while she was unconscious."

"That's a good idea," Cassie said, kissing him.

Hannah watched them wistfully.

"I'll go see about some travel arrangements," Paul said. "Either of you ladies need anything?"

"No thanks, Paul."

Cassie plunked herself down on the couch next to Hannah. "This is a different side of him," Hannah said.

"I know that you don't really think he's right for me, but he's good to me and he's been a rock through all this. When the authorities called me to inform me of your accident, I didn't know what to do. I was so upset. I feel like this was all my fault, leaving you to travel on your own. This wouldn't have happened if we'd been together. I kinda lost it. But he made all the travel arrangements and kept in touch with the police and the hospital. He had everything arranged for when we got here. He's just been here for me. And you too."

"Yeah. I appreciate that. Everything you've both done. I envy you, Cassidy."

Cassie turned to her, shock crossing her features. Hannah had never liked Paul or the fact that he and Cass were together. And Cass was very aware of it.

"I envy what you have with him. I wish..." Hannah dissolved into a fresh bout of tears. Hannah was not prone to tears and that was all she'd done the past few days.

Cass pulled her into her arms. "Hannie? Did he hurt you? The guy? I mean, the docs never said that you were assaulted—ya know, raped or anything—but you have bruises like fingerprints on your breasts, they said. Can you remember?"

"No, Lock did that. Don't worry. He didn't hurt me. He's just a little aggressive. I actually learned to enjoy that."

"You think you had sex with this guy? This *Lock* guy that you think you remember?"

"Yes."

"This guy that you met in Wales?"

Hannah nodded, knowing by the tone of Cassie's voice where this conversation was headed, just like all the others in the last few days. Back to no one believing her. *Let's face it—I'm beginning to doubt myself.*

Cassie shook her head. "Did you meet him in the pub in Llandeilo?" Cassie's voice grew with anger.

"No, I didn't meet him at the pub. I never went down to the pub. I don't think..." Why couldn't she grab onto a thought and keep it? All of her memories were jumbled up with what she could barely remember, things she couldn't remember happening at all and Cassie's version of events. What was real?

"Hannah. The only man besides Jake that you met here hurt you and would have done worse if Jake hadn't happened by. Maybe you met him at the pub. Perhaps you were having a good time with him. Flirting. Dancing, having a few drinks? Possibly even doing a little more than that? Conceivably, you're just getting things confused with him because just maybe you were into him, in the bar. You could have even thought about screwing him for one night and things got out of hand. You changed your mind. He was pissed and he followed you outside. If you met this Lock at the pub and he's the one that grabbed you hard enough to bruise you, then he's the one that did this to you. *He* hurt you. So stop trying to make him out to be some kind of hero that you need to find because in your mind you had a high time with him. You didn't."

"Lock didn't do this to me. How do I know he isn't hurt, too? We were in Scotland the last time I saw him."

"Don't get yourself all worked up again. Here. I'll show you the pictures you sent me." Cassie opened her laptop.

"I sent you pictures? I don't remember sending you anything." As Hannah remembered it, she'd been so pissed off at Cassie for cancelling at the last minute that she purposely hadn't sent her any pictures or emails.

"Look, here's the first one, a photo from the plane as it descended. Even the caption sounded excited. '*Look, Cass, English soil*', you said. Then there's a picture of the hotel we were supposed to stay in together. I think you were trying to rub it in a little there. I actually thought you'd come home, Hannie. I didn't think you'd come all this way alone. It's not like you. You try to act tough, but I know better."

"But you knew how much this trip meant to me."

Her friend sighed. "I know how important it is to you *now*," she said uneasily. "I guess I really didn't realise how much coming here meant to you."

"But this isn't something new, Cass. I've always wanted to come here, especially since I lost my mum. You knew that."

"It's no excuse, Hannah, I'm sorry, but I guess I've just been so preoccupied with Paul that I just didn't think."

"Don't be. I get it now. I understand what it's like to be all caught up in someone else. It's all you want, all the time."

Cassie watched her closely before scrolling to the next photo.

"Here's some cute guys you thought I'd like. Oh, and this one of the guy in the kilt with the caption that reads '*Help me out, Cass, shaggable? I think so!*' Paul didn't seem to find the humour in that one."

"I really don't remember sending that."

"Here's the day you took the bus trip to see the castles and the next day when you went to see the cathedrals."

Hannah watched the slideshow. It was as much a blur in her mind as it looked on the screen. She vaguely recalled some of these things, but she didn't remember it all and she did not recollect sending the emails.

"This was shopping day in London when you bought the *Kiss Me, I'm Scottish* T-shirt. Oh, and Paul did like this one." She flipped to that picture. Hannah looked at the picture of herself with the T-shirt knotted tightly under her breasts, showing off her midriff, wearing only a pair of panties for bottoms.

"Why would you show him that?" Hannah asked, embarrassed, sliding her finger over the mouse pad, successfully flipping to the next image.

"Why did you take it?"

"I don't remember taking it, to be honest, and why did I send it to *you*?"

"Who were you going to send it to? Gerard?" she teased.

Hannah perked up as in her mind's eye she saw Lock looking down at her with one thing on his mind. *'Is the sayin' on your chemise the truth then, lass? Because true or no, I am goin' to kiss ya.'* Then some time later he'd demanded, *'Kiss me, lass, I'm Scottish.'*

"Wait! I met Lock in that T-shirt."

"Where were you?"

"Um…I was…we were…" She couldn't say for certain but for some reason she clearly remembered him removing the T-shirt and admiring her bra and panties. *'What are these that you wear?'*

"Scotland?" Cassie asked impatiently. "Or outside the pub in Llandeilo?"

"I can't remember where we were."

"Look, Han, here's the picture of the house your mom grew up in."

Hannah touched the screen reverently. "I don't remember that. Did I go there?"

"You wrote that you wished you could have seen the place with your mom, and you even took a photo of the street sign. You said it would have to be enough."

"It would have to be enough? I said that?" She remembered saying that, but to Lockhart for some reason. "I can't recall."

"Oh, and this one's funny, too. Look at you and this guy at the foot of the London Eye. He looks like he's into you. And this next one's a riot. Somehow you convinced him to tie up his T-shirt just like you'd done in the naughty picture. Then, look, you've both got your shirts hiked up, and you must have had someone else take the picture because you two are on the opposite seat in the gondola as you rode the wheel. He has his arm around you. Look how happy you look, Hannah. Could that guy be Lock? Maybe this is the guy you had sex with, in London, before you even came to Wales, and your mind is just playing tricks on you because of the knock on the head? Perhaps that was the guy you were going to send that other photo to. Maybe you did."

Hannah stared at the guy, who must have been just another random sightseer. He had on one of those T-shirts with the print of a camera on it, like it was hanging around his neck, clearly announcing he was a tourist. "No, that's not Lock. I don't remember posing for this. I asked a guy to take my picture? That can't be right. I never went up in the wheel." She shook her head in frustration. "I don't know, I just don't know." She scraped her lip with her teeth, trying to conjure not only Lockhart but what objects and scenery were around him at the time. Possibly then she might remember where they'd been.

Hannah pointed at the picture. "You say after this, I came to Wales," Hannah wanted to clarify.

Cassie nodded. "Just like we'd planned. A week in London, which you clearly did." She waved over the laptop and the evidence therein. "You took the bus and obviously got off. There was some mix-up with the ticket to Swansea — evidently you needed to make a transfer. The ticket booth was closed. You were alone, at night, in the dark, in probably not the best part of town..."

"I remember going to Wales," Hannah said, remembering leaning her head against the glass as she'd seriously considered going home. "It was raining."

"Yes, that's right. Jake said as much when we went to pick up your bags. He said it was an awful night."

She closed her eyes again. "You say Jake lives in a flat with his gran. But I clearly see Lock in their kitchen." She shivered as she thought of how he'd made her feel when he'd laid her back on the scarred old table in the farmhouse kitchen. "Yes, that's where I met him." She clasped Cassie's arm. "I met him at Jake's."

"No, Hannie, you didn't." She shook her head sadly. "You never went to Jake's place. There is no farmhouse that looks like a castle. You got off the bus and promptly went to the hospital. That's where you've been and that's where you've stayed until you woke up and Paul and I were here."

Hannah's head began to pound with every heartbeat. She stood and paced. "I went to Wales. I missed the last bus. Jake and his gran took pity on me and they took me to their house. I met Lock and we rented a van and we went to his place in Scotland."

"No. You. Didn't," Cassie said firmly.

"Yes, I did. *We* did," Hannah reiterated.

"Hannah, you're really starting to freak me out. What the fuck's wrong with you? This Lock does not exist. If he's not the guy that attacked you, then what is he? Some kind of ghost or something that came to you while you were in a coma?"

Hannah's mind swirled. She saw Lockhart step out of the portrait. And that was all she saw before the blackness enveloped her.

* * * *

Hannah awoke to Cassie and Paul speaking quietly.

"Try not to worry, Cass. The doctor said she might have these kinds of spells for a while. We need to get her home, to her own physician. She might even need someone to talk to."

Hannah sat up. "You two can go home." She tried to stand but the pain in her forehead kept her down. "Go home. I'm staying."

"You are not staying here!" Cassie crossed her arms. "I let you get hurt here once, I'll be damned if I'll allow you stay here in the condition you're in."

Hannah stood shakily. "I have to go to Scotland, Cass. I have to. I need to see for myself that he's…that he's…" Hannah sat back down heavily. See that he was what? Safe? Alive? Real? What was it she felt she really needed to do? Or did she need to know for herself that she was crazy?

"Hannah, for fuck's sake! He doesn't exist outside of your mind. You never met this guy. You don't *need* to see anything."

"And that's why you should go home," Hannah shot back. "Because you don't believe me. I can't go back home until I'm sure."

"Hannah, you have yourself believing that you've been here three days more than you have. That you spent days with some guy that may or may not have been the man that hurt you. I want to go home. Let's go. This place has brought you nothing but pain. I want you home where you can heal."

"I have to know, Cassie. What don't you understand? I won't be able to heal until I know. He was real. He was real to me." Or maybe he wasn't. Maybe he was a ghost. But she couldn't tell Cassie that was what she thought she remembered. And why had a ghost needed her to rent a van so that they could transport…something? Perhaps she was crazy, but she felt this heart-pulling need to go back to Scotland or she would never be able to reconcile fact from fiction. "I'm going back."

Cassie threw her hands in the air. "Where in Scotland are you going to go?"

"Good question," Hannah mumbled.

"Do you even know? You don't, do you? That's kinda vast, don't you think? Just *Scotland*."

"I'll find out where I rented the van. They will have records as to where their van went."

"You never rented a goddamn van, Hannah."

"Yes, I did." Her eyes widened as she remembered Jake being with her when she did and also how he'd given her a quick driving lesson. "Jake was with me."

"No, he *wasn't!*"

"Cass," Paul cautioned, speaking quietly. "Ease up on her. She's confused. It's not her fault. Yelling at her is not going to help. Look," he said to Hannah, "why don't I give Jake a call? We'll ask him. He's a nice kid. I know he'll want to help. Would that make you feel better, Hannah?"

117

Paul placed the call. Jake agreed to come over to the hotel and see her in person.

"Why don't you go wash your face and brush your hair, Han, before he gets here," Cass suggested.

Hannah obediently went into the bathroom and washed her face, careful to pat it dry. She looked into the mirror at the bruise on her cheekbone that was beginning to fade. She had no idea where it had come from, or the abrasion on her chin. Had she really been attacked? Had she totally dreamt Lockhart?

"No, he loved me," she said to her reflection. "He said so."

She pulled down the front of her shirt and looked at the fading fingerprints on her chest. She didn't want them to heal. They were the only proof she had of him.

She brushed her hair and pulled it into a ponytail. Paul and Cass had their heads together when she exited.

"Can I use your laptop?" Hannah asked.

"Sure."

Hannah took it and searched the names of Scottish towns, hoping something might jump out at her or seem familiar and she would know where to go. But she had no such luck.

His house had a name. What was it? Her head began to ache again. She couldn't even remember his last name. She typed Lockhart into the search bar and a mere thirty-four and a half million results listed. She began to look through them, hoping something might twig her memory.

There was a slight knock at the door. She moved the laptop and stood, almost feeling relief at the thought of seeing Jake. A kid of about eighteen or nineteen walked into the room. He smiled at Hannah. She looked past him waiting to see Jake.

"Hannah," Paul said softly. "You remember Jake?"

"I was surprised to hear you remembered me at all, miss. You seemed to be unconscious the entire time."

Hannah's stomach rolled. Cass took her arm firmly to steady her. "What is it?"

"That's not Jake!" Hannah whispered, incredulously, allowing Cass to lower her into a chair. Cassie and Paul exchanged another look as the poor kid's face fell.

Hannah cupped her forehead with her hand. "What's happening to me?"

Hannah just heard snippets of their conversation after that. *Rented van…unconscious…she swears she met a man in your kitchen…medics…*

"My pin!" Hannah blurted, taking Cassie's hand tightly. "My red maple leaf pin. I gave it to the real Jake. I pinned it on his jacket myself."

The boy shook his head slowly, watching her with a curious, pity-filled stare.

Hannah closed her eyes. Was none of it real? A dream? Had she fallen in love with a dream? Was it something she'd wanted so much that her subconscious had invented the perfect man for her?

Cassie handed Hannah two yellow and white capsules and a glass of water. Hannah swallowed them dutifully then crawled back into the bed.

Chapter Twelve

Hannah sat across the table from Paul and Cassidy in the hotel restaurant the next morning. Hannah pushed her food around the plate.

Three plane tickets sat in the middle of the table.

"I have to get back to work," Paul explained. "I can't take any more time off."

Hannah raised tired eyes to him. She'd been feeling dopey ever since Cassie had started feeding her pills every four hours. She felt lazy and lethargic. She didn't give a shit about anything. She didn't want to leave the UK but she didn't want to stay alone. She wanted to go home but she didn't know why—there was nothing there for her. Lockhart was here. Somewhere. Or wasn't he? Was he here? Or was he dead? Or had he never even existed outside of her mind?

Paul picked up one of the tickets and slid it into his inside chest pocket. "You girls make sure you stick together." He smiled.

"Thanks for understanding, babe," Cassie patted his chest. "I think she just needs to see for herself. But I don't feel right about just abandoning her."

"And I don't want you to. I feel like some of this is my fault, too. If I hadn't pressured you to stay with me instead of taking this trip, maybe none of this would have happened to Hannah. You two have been planning this voyage longer than I've been around. I shouldn't have stopped you. You still have two weeks left of vacation time—you may as well take it."

Hannah nodded, no longer sure that she would find anything, but she appreciated the sincerity that she saw in his blue eyes. He pushed the other two tickets closer to Hannah. "It's a thirty-six minute flight from Cardiff to Glasgow. I hope you find what you need, Hannah."

Her eyes filled. "Thank you, Paul, for everything you've done."

His mouth twisted. "I've gotta go or I'll miss my flight." He stood and kissed Cassie soundly. "I'll see you beautiful ladies in a couple of weeks. I love you, babe," he said, leaning in and kissing Cassie again.

I love you, Hannah-lass, Lockhart's distinctive brogue purred through her hazy consciousness.

"Keep in touch and be careful," Paul said, looking at Cass with love and concern.

For the life of her, Hannah couldn't remember why she hadn't liked Paul. He was a good guy.

After he left, Cassie looked across the table and handed Hannah a napkin to dry her face with. "Well, let's get packed up and we'll get ourselves to Cardiff so we can catch our flight. Any idea what we're looking for once we land? Or if we'll find it in Glasgow?" she asked hopefully as she set two more capsules in front of her.

"Well, if you quit shoving those down my throat I might be able to think clearly."

"Hannah, you haven't had a clear thought since you woke up."

"So you say."

"Maybe you don't think so, but you're better off on them, for now."

"What are they anyway?" Hannah asked, as she swilled them down with the water. "Some kind of antidepressant?"

Cassie looked levelly across the table at her. "They are anti-psychotics."

They suddenly felt like a lump in Hannah's throat. "You think I've had some kind of psychotic break? You think I came here and now suddenly I'm what...schizophrenic?"

"Are you hearing voices?" she shot back.

Hannah couldn't deny that. She was sure that she heard Lockhart speaking to her.

"Do you think you saw a ghost or two, since you swear Jake isn't even Jake? And then there is the disappearing Lock. Look, Hannah, I think you've had a traumatic experience and you just don't know quite how to deal with it yet."

"So you think a pill is going to fix it for me?"

"The pills first and then when we get you home, we'll find you a good psychiatrist to talk to and you'll be just fine. Now, come on. Let's get on with this mission to nowhere. I personally would like to get home and put this all behind us. And you should want that, too."

* * * *

Cassie and Hannah stood in a very short line of people waiting to get onto the small Jetstream that would take them to Glasgow.

"I hope they have hard liquor on this flight," Cass said, looking anxiously outside at the plane.

"Why?" Hannah asked, disinterestedly.

"Does it look to you like that thing is going to stay in the air? I mean really, it looks like an antique, for Christ's sake. Was it built after the Second World War or what?"

Hannah shrugged. Who cared? So what if it went down? Nothing mattered. Why was she even going through with this? Cassie was right – it was a mission to nowhere. The more time that passed, the foggier her memories got. She was even beginning to lose sight of Lock's handsome face. He was fading, just like her bruises.

"I'm gonna go check on our bags. I can still see them sitting in the exact same place that we left them. Wouldn't that just be a capper on this vacation disaster from hell you've got going on here, if we lost our luggage, too? Stay here," Cassie finished sternly, making her feel like a wandering child.

Hannah scrubbed her hand down her face. She felt numb. Tingly. She could touch her thumb and forefinger together and not even feel it. *Is it the drugs?* She felt like she wasn't even there. Like things were going on around her and she was not included. Life was like a dream now. Everything felt unreal.

Hannah looked up at the line of people ahead of her. Her eyes felt heavy. She rubbed them tiredly. Screw it. They might as well just go home. There was nothing here for her. This was useless.

Hannah opened her eyes and was about to turn when a man in the front of the line caught her eye. He was a head taller than everyone else around him. Short dark hair. Broad shoulders. Chiselled body. Hannah's skin leapt with energy. Perfectly sculpted face complete with a slight cleft in the chin. He took his sunglasses off and slid them up into his hair, uncovering familiar dark eyes.

"Lock?" she breathed, as her heart pounded loudly. She felt more alive than she had since she woke up. "Lock?" she repeated, stronger this time, moving in his direction, unable to stop herself. He looked amazing in modern clothing. A brown T-shirt hugged his rippling muscles over low-slung, tight-fitting faded jeans.

She seized his arm. "Lock?"

He looked down at her in surprise. "Yes," he answered, but she could see that there was no recognition of her. She looked more closely. It was him but it wasn't. Her heart raced but it hurt with every beat. Her mind swirled numbly from the medication, making her unable to process thought quickly. She wavered dizzily. He took hold of her elbows and pulled her against him trying to keep her upright. As soon as their bodies touched a current of sexual energy shot through them.

"Whoa!" He felt it too—she was sure. "What the hell? Are you all right, miss?"

"Lock?" she breathed.

"Aye, do I know ya?" His dark brows dove as his eyes searched hers. "Have we met?"

They stared at each other until finally Hannah couldn't stand not feeling his lips on hers. She thrust her hands into his hair and pulled his head down towards her. He didn't resist her. His lips parted, as she'd known they would. He bent to meet her.

"Hannah! What are you doing?" Cassie wrenched her backward just as she was about to feel his lips.

"Lock! It's Lock!" Hannah choked, trying to explain the overwhelming need she felt.

Cassie turned cold, assessing eyes on him. "Are you?" she asked, bluntly.

"Aye," he answered, "Llachlan. Llachlan Munro," he introduced himself and presented his hand, which Cassie ignored.

"Do you know her?" Cassie asked, hands on hips.

"I'm not sure. She seems to know me."

"Were you going to take advantage of her again? You didn't know her at the pub either."

"Take advantage? Again? I've no idea what ya are gettin' at. At what pub? And I believe I was the one bein' taken advantage of just now." His accent came out more pronounced the more agitated he grew.

"I didn't see you fending her off!" Cassie retorted, turning to Hannah, who stood staring up at him. "Oh, fer fuck! Come on! I can't leave you alone for a second now, can I?" Cassie dragged her back to their place in line. "What the fuck is wrong with you?"

"It's Lock."

"It's not fuckin' Lock!" Cass gritted irritably. "He doesn't exist and if he does then he's the one that hurt you! What don't you understand?"

"He said he was…"

"He would have said anything to keep you going at him like you were. He's a guy, after all. Like he's gonna turn you down when you're all over him like that? Honestly, you've lost all sense."

Hannah couldn't keep her eyes off him and he seemed to be having the same problem. Their gazes kept colliding.

Munro, he'd said. Llachlan Munro. Could that be it? Lockhart Munro? He looked so much like Lockhart. They had to be related. Lockhart Munro from…where? She racked her drug-fogged brain. His house had a name. *It started with a…T…*

"Tamworth, Trent, Trafalgar…" Hannah said, out loud. "Tr…Traf-something…" She shook her head.

"What are you doing now?" Cassie asked in frustration.

"What other names in the UK do you know that begin with T-R?"

"You know, I am seriously thinking of putting you in a straitjacket and dropping you off at the nearest monastery for an exorcism."

The line started to move, loading the passengers onto the small aircraft.

Cassie pointed to their seats then pulled the overhead compartment open and tossed her case inside. Hannah lifted her own over her head to do the same, but she felt so weak and tired, it tipped backward and would have toppled down onto her head if a large hand hadn't appeared and stopped it.

"Here now. Let me help ya with that," his deep burr purred just near Hannah's ear, sending heat lancing through her body. She allowed herself to relax against his hard chest as he reached around her and stuffed the bag into the cubicle. It wasn't the only hard thing she felt. He was responding to her. She spun around to place her palms on his ribs. She searched his face. She wanted desperately for him to know her. "Please…" she pleaded.

His dark eyes were puzzled as he looked down at her. "Please what, lass?"

An attendant walked down the aisle instructing them to take their seats. Cassie took the opportunity to shove Hannah into the window seat as she took the aisle.

The engines roared, making the fuselage shudder and shake. Cassie gripped the armrests as the plane took off and eventually levelled out. She looked across the aisle. "Look. I'm sorry if I overreacted back there. My friend has recently suffered a trauma. A head injury, actually, and she's just not acting like herself."

"Am I not here?" Hannah snapped, pissed off with Cassie's insensitivity.

"It's no trouble," he commented. "It's kind of ironic actually. I've also suffered an accident that resulted in a head wound recently myself. So, yeah, this is entirely strange," he said, nodding. He sat back in his seat trying to make room for his long legs. "Where are you headed?" he enquired.

"To Glasgow. On a wild goose chase," Cassie responded snidely.

He raised a dark brow. "Oh?"

"She believes she's lost something in Scotland. A place she's never actually set foot in." The plane suddenly hit a patch of turbulence. When the shaking stopped, Cassie stood. "I'm going to see if there is any alcohol on this bucket of bolts. *You*, stay!" she said, pointing to Hannah condescendingly.

Llachlan ran a hand through his hair as he watched the mouthy blonde walk up the aisle, then turned his attention back to the pretty brunette with the incredible, beseeching green eyes. She sat in the seat with her head bowed, her eyes downcast, her lips moving as if she were praying, perhaps. He remembered those early days, trying to figure out what was real and what was imagined. Trying to get used to the medication, which was so strong that it wiped out all feeling, good or bad. It was like walking through a fog.

He didn't know what to say but he wanted to reach out to her. She seemed so lost and alone. And achingly familiar to him. She was beautiful. He'd thought so the minute he'd caught sight of her in the line and hadn't been able to keep his eyes off her. He felt drawn to her but couldn't think of a logical reason to approach or a stupid line to use when he got there. But he didn't want to play games. He'd recently come to the conclusion life was too short for that shit.

"What's your name, English?" he began, then belatedly wondered why he'd addressed her as such. It was not something he would normally say. But then again, many things he'd done and said in the last little while didn't make any sense, and he'd stopped trying to make them so.

He saw a tear fall down her cheek and it made his chest hurt. "I'm Canadian," she whispered, almost rocking in the seat.

"That's a strange name," he chuckled, in a poor attempt at humour.

"No, my name is Hannah. I'm from Canada. Are you a dumb ghost?"

The minute she said her name he heard nothing else. A bolt of electricity shot through him. "Hannah," he repeated, her name bursting from his lips before he could stop it, as if for a split second he had no control over his thoughts or his mouth. For a moment he had not been in control of his own faculties.

It's Hannah and don't you forget it... he heard her say from somewhere far away. Another woman. Another time. It was her but it wasn't her. He fisted his hands on the armrests, trying to stave off the cloud of darkness that he knew would come next. Why did he keep hearing and seeing these things? Things and people he didn't know. *Not now,* he implored.

Her head snapped around and in her glistening eyes he saw the same terror-stricken panic that he felt. He released his fists, and his hands shook. His palms were wet as he slid them over his denim-clad thighs. He faced forward in his seat.

"Hannah," he said again, trying to speak her name casually. Making sure that he was again in control of his lips. But something still resonated in the plane's cabin as if it echoed. "It suits you," he said, trying to hold his thoughts. There were times when he thought he was doing okay, then something would happen to prove him wrong. He didn't want to have an episode now, in front of her. He needed to pull off this trip without incident and show himself and his parents that he was going to be all right. He'd already kept the episode he'd had last week a secret from everyone, or they never would have let him set off on this trip alone. And he definitely didn't share the fact that his first night away, he'd found himself in an alleyway in Wales. Inexplicable. More lost time.

Out of the corner of his eye he saw Hannah cover her face with her hands. "Okay," she said. "I get it. You're not really here. Maybe I'm not even here."

Llachlan covered his own eyes trying to keep the blackness at bay.

"Oh, look at you two," Cassie said, throwing herself into the seat as vapours of recently consumed liquor followed her. "Are we bonding over missing brain cells?"

Hannah turned hurt-filled eyes on her friend and stood. "You know what, Cassidy, sometimes you can be a real bitch!"

She was about to leave and Llach couldn't stand the thought of her not being near him. He was loath to let her out of his sight, still fighting the darkness that was threatening. He reached for her hand. She immediately coiled her fingers around his as if he were her lifeline. Another blast of sexual heat slammed into him. *Fuck! What is that?* He wanted this woman, this stranger. He wanted her under him, on top of him, going down on him, crawling all over him. He could almost see it, feel it—he could smell her, he could taste her. He wanted to grab her and crush his lips to hers. His emotions were so erratic lately. He was impulsive and unpredictable. He never knew what to expect from himself anymore and this inexplicable, painful attraction he had for her just might prove his undoing.

He shook his head trying to clear it. "I know what you're goin' through," he said, looking up at her. "Never knowing what's real or imaginary. Feeling like no one believes anything you say. Wondering if you can believe yourself, your own thoughts and actions. My family share memories that I have no recollection of but they insist I was there when these things happened. I've had people I've known all my life come up to me and I don't know them. That's why when ya touched me I asked if I knew ya. I honestly don't know anymore." He moved over to the next seat, pulling her down beside him.

A tear streaked down her cheek. His chest tightened at the sight of it. He resisted the urge to reach out and catch it.

"The worst is the lost time," he continued.

"Lost time?" she whispered. Her luminescent green eyes searched his.

"Aye. Blackouts, they tell me. I do and I say things, and I don't remember doing or saying them. Or I imagine things that are not. I dream people I don't even know. I wake up in places that I did not go to sleep in and have no recollection of how I got there. Have ya experienced this?"

"Yes. I lost three days," she said. He found himself spellbound by her accent and the sound of her voice. He could smell a hint of vanilla, from her shampoo he guessed, and he found himself inhaling deeply trying to absorb it into himself.

"But I feel like I lived more in those three days than I have my whole life," she continued. "And now I just want to go back and live those three days over and over." Her full bottom lip trembled. He wanted to reach out and trace that lovely lip with his thumb. What if she'd kissed him earlier? He wouldn't have stopped her. Surely he would have been arrested for what would come next. Because he knew that kissing her would be explosive. He felt his blood rushing even now and he was having difficulty breathing properly just thinking about it and being this close to her.

He swallowed hard. "I know what ya mean. And your friend there" — he pointed at Cassie who watched and listened intently — "she is a little overprotective, yeah?" Llachlan struggled to make his voice sound normal.

Hannah shrugged delicately. "She's just trying to save me from myself, I guess."

Cassie snorted. "And it's a full-time job, too."

"My parents were the same with me," he continued. "They didn't want me to take this trip. At least not on my own. But I needed to. I had to prove to them and to myself that I could without some big disaster happening. I'm actually surprised that I haven't turned around to find my brother sneaking around behind me just to make sure that I'm okay. It would be just like them."

Hannah softened. "Because they love you. They won't ever give up on you. Especially your father. So don't you give up on yourself." She said these things as if she knew. Her eyes brightened a little and it was like the sun came out. "You did it? You accomplished your goal?" It was her way of asking if he was just beginning his trip or ending it.

"It would seem so."

"You took this excursion all on your own, and nothing bad has happened. You're going to be fine." Her beautiful mouth moved into a real smile, and his heart pounded faster at the sight. "I'm proud of you, Lock."

The way she said his name seemed so familiar. It wasn't just that he was attracted to her. It was more than that. There was no denying the sexual tension they had going on. She sparked something in him the minute she'd touched him. His cock had been hard ever since she'd attempted to kiss him. But there was something else. A connection that he didn't want to break. She made him feel good when nothing had made him feel that way since the accident.

"It must feel so good for you to be out and about moving freely after so long." Her gaze never wavered from his, as if she could see right inside him. Her eyes packed a punch that reached right into his chest. She looked at him like she had feelings for him. Deep feelings. Like a lover.

He took his hand, the one she wasn't clinging to, and pulled at his trouser leg, attempting to readjust himself, trying to ease the pressure on his straining cock.

"May I ask, was your trip for pleasure?" Her attention strayed from his for the first time, dipping to his mouth, making his tongue venture out to wet his parched lips. "Or was it a business?" Her eyes were even hotter when they rejoined his.

He cleared his throat. "It was a business trip. I went to acquire a piece of art for our collection."

"A piece of art?" she said, slowly.

"A portrait, actually."

She paled visibly. "A portrait?"

"Aye, we have a gallery."

"Would it be a full-scale portrait?"

"Yes," he answered, trying to interpret her strange reaction.

A quiver shook her small frame. "Did you acquire it in Wales?" she enquired, softly.

His eyes narrowed. "Aye, how do ya know all this?"

Hannah turned and looked to her friend, who shook her head in warning.

He wished that Hannah would just stand up to her friend, Cassie. It was the medication subduing her. He was sure. He'd been through it himself. Just went along with what everyone told him to do in that fog that just pushed you along. But he'd seen a bit of spark in her when she'd called Cassie a bitch. He thought maybe he'd seen a flash of what the real Hannah might be like.

"Please return to your seat and put on your seat belt, Miss. We are about to land," an attendant said to Hannah from the aisle.

Llachlan blocked her exit with his arm. He couldn't shake the uncomfortable notion of her leaving his side. Not even for a second. He took the ends of the seatbelt and connected them. As he moved to pull away his pinkie finger caught in the little flap covering the zipper of the capris she wore and slightly grazed her. Her lips parted, and that same sizzling heat shot between them.

His eyes met hers. He had to utilise every ounce of control that he still possessed to resist the urge he felt to ram his hand between her legs and cup the sweet treat in his hand. He almost knew that she would be receptive. She would push her crotch more fully into his palm, seeking his touch. He growled low in his chest as vicious need to bury himself between her thighs slammed into him. He felt like an animal — primitive, instinctive, carnal. He wanted her. Simple. Man. Woman. Fuck. And it didn't help that he saw the same mindless desire in her eyes.

"Lock?" she said, his name in question as her gaze searched his. What was she looking for? Whatever it was, he wanted to give it to her.

The plane started its descent. Llach shifted reluctantly back in the seat, fastening his own safety belt. She held her hand out to him, palm up, trusting. He laid his palm against hers, threading his fingers through hers. He closed his eyes and tried to concentrate on the sound of the plane instead of the hunger that was making his skin leap with excitement and anticipation. When they landed, the bitchy blonde would take her away from him. How was he going to stop that from happening? At the very least he wanted to know where he could find her. He had to see her again. He needed it like he needed to breathe.

Hannah's mind reeled. Nothing made sense. He was Lockhart but he wasn't. He sounded like him. He moved like him. He even smelt like him.

When she looked into his eyes, she felt like he was there, just beyond her reach. He made her feel like

Lockhart did. He felt it too. She knew that he did. Why didn't he know her? Why didn't he recognise her? He was there, inside this Llachlan. She had to bring him out somehow.

The plane landed and she racked her brain for some excuse to stay with him. She needed more time.

Cassie grabbed her as soon as they touched down. "Come on. We need to find a room."

"What's the hurry?" Hannah sulked.

"I've got a buzz that I'd like to keep."

Hannah followed reluctantly as Cassie opened the overhead compartment.

"Allow me," Llachlan said, standing, taking out Cassie's case and handing it to her. He reached for Hannah's. He passed it to her, keeping his hands on it even after he knew that it was securely in her grasp. "You don't have a hotel room yet?"

"No," she said, softly looking up at him.

His lips tightened. "I could make some suggestions," he offered.

"That would be helpful…"

"We'll manage, thanks, Braveheart," Cassie said nastily. She took hold of Hannah's case and gave it a quick jerk. "And you can quit hitting on her. It's not gonna happen, stud."

He followed them out onto the tarmac. "I'm only trying to help. You have no idea what she's goin' through. If you could just give us some time together?"

"Oh, well then, it would be in everyone's best interest if I left her in your capable hands, right?" Cassie responded, sarcastically. "Because you know exactly what she's going through. You know precisely what she needs. Now, what kind of friend would I be if I left her with a complete stranger? The exact stranger, in fact, that she, at least, believes is the last person to see her before she was attacked on the street. Yeah, not gonna happen, buddy. Go prey on some other unsuspecting woman."

Llachlan's concerned gaze shot to Hannah. "You were attacked? That's what happened to ya?"

Hannah shook her head and shrugged, embarrassed and even more unsure of what had happened to her.

Llachlan saw his brother approaching them. He knew that he would be just as overly protective on his behalf as Cassie was for Hannah. Malcolm would want to know every little detail from the trip and if he'd had any problems. "Can I give ya my number?" Llach rushed. "Ya can call me. If ya want to," he added.

Hannah nodded. He reached into his back pocket and opened his wallet, taking out his card. He placed it into her hand. "Don't lose it, yeah?"

"I won't," she whispered, gazing back at him longingly as Cassie pulled her along.

"Wait!" Hannah lunged for Llachlan, wrapping her hands around his forearms tightly. She looked up at him, her eyes almost wild. "The portrait? Please! Tell me. Is it Lockhart Munro?"

Llachlan's eyebrows dove in surprise as the hair on the back of his neck stood up.

"Aye, but how could you…know?"

Her eyes closed and she bit her bottom lip as her friend pulled her from his grasp. His brother, Malcolm, reached him then and the barrage of questions started. "Hey, Llach, how was the trip? Have any problems? Did you get the paintin'?"

"No problems. It was good," he answered, distractedly watching Hannah disappear.

"Who was that?" his brother asked, lifting a curious brow.

"We don't know her?" Llachlan asked, just to make sure.

"Not that I know of. Why, do you think you do?"

He shrugged. He felt like he did. "I don't know. I feel like I know her." He wanted to know her.

"Are ya feelin' okay?" Malcolm asked, deep concern creasing his brow.

"Yes, I'm fine. I wish everyone would stop askin' me that! Let's just get that portrait loaded and get home." And then he would try and find out how she knew about the painting.

Chapter Thirteen

Hannah and Cassie settled at a Hilton in Glasgow. Cassie was nursing her third rum and Coke while Hannah feverishly searched online for Llachlan. And trying to narrow down a Llachlan Munro in Scotland was like trying to find a Bill Smith or J. Jones in Canada.

She would just look at the card he'd given her if Cassie hadn't yanked it out of her hand and shoved it into her purse. Hannah was just happy that she hadn't ripped it up and tossed it.

"Chug it, Cass, and I'll freshen your drink," Hannah encouraged.

"Oh, you are so sweet, Han. At least that hasn't changed."

"Yes, Cassie, and you're one of those drunks that loves everyone," Hannah said, doubling the rum, adding only a splash of Coke.

"Hey, Hannie, why don't we get all tramped up and go out to one of the pubs, just like we planned?"

"Mmm, I don't think pubs and anti-psychotics go well together."

"Oh, shit! Right. You probably shouldn't drink. Well, then you can just watch me have a good time. You can still drink Coke and dance with the hunky Highlanders."

"No, the pills just make me tired. I think I'll just go to bed."

"Oh, you're no fun, Hannah-banana," she pouted. She reached into her purse and tossed the bottle of pills at Hannah. "That reminds me — you should take those. Do you think I should sleep with one eye open?" she said, laughing too loudly.

"Well, I don't know, but if you can do that, maybe you'd better. You never know when I might snap. Drink up."

Hannah didn't feel good about what she was doing, but she made sure Cassie's drink was endless. Cassie was one of those people that drank one night and then spent the whole next day paying for it. She'd be in bed with a headache and puking all day tomorrow, and that was just what Hannah wanted. A day to herself.

When Cassie finally passed out, Hannah pulled her friend's legs up onto the couch and covered her up. She went into her purse and pulled out Llachlan's card. Three things jumped out at her all at once. Llachlan, Airdrie and Trafalis. "Trafalis. Trafalis Hall," she repeated. That was the T-R word she was looking for. That was all she needed.

Hannah got ready for bed. She didn't take the pills, hoping that she would be able to think more clearly once they cleared her system. She tried desperately to remember her days with Lockhart. Had they actually driven to Trafalis Hall together? Was that his home? And what was it that they had needed to take there? And why had he been so adamant about it? She needed to see for herself.

* * * *

The next day, Hannah wrote Cassie a note so that she wouldn't worry, then she rented a car and headed for Airdrie. She typed the coordinates for Trafalis Hall into the GPS. According to the positioning system, it was only twenty kilometres and about twenty-six minutes' driving time.

As she drove, she tried to pick out anything that might look familiar. Nothing did. No landmarks, not even the names on the signs seemed to tickle anything in her memory. Was Trafalis Hall Lockhart's home? Was she even remembering that correctly? Had they driven here?

"So start at the beginning," she said to herself. "What do I absolutely know is fact? I flew to England. I did touristy things, but don't remember sending Cassie photos. I took a bus to Wales, then what? I was either attacked and spent three days unconscious, or I went to a different Jake's farmhouse and had mad amazing sex with a guy that may or may not have stepped out of a portrait of himself. And he was Lockhart Munro, who may or may not be a ghost." She shook her head. "But it doesn't make sense. If I was in the hospital and it was all a dream, then why do I even know that a portrait of Lockhart Munro even exists?" And she knew now for sure that it did because Llachlan had confirmed that he was indeed in possession of the portrait that he had acquired in Wales. How could she have known that?

And what of Llachlan? He was so much like Lockhart in so many ways—it had been difficult for her to be near him and not touch him and kiss him the way that she wanted to. She had to keep reminding herself that he was not Lockhart. But when he'd growled low in his chest, when he'd touched her, it had been as if he was. Her body had reacted to the sound and his touch and something had passed in his eyes that made her believe for a split second that he knew her. That Lockhart was in this man.

She shook her head. "You only want Lockhart to be there," she said out loud.

Trafalis Hall came into view. She drove up the long, winding drive and parked the car. She stepped out and looked at the ruin that had once been a castle. Fluorescent tape warned *Beware, Keep Out, No Trespassing*.

She felt inexplicable disappointment. It was not what she'd been expecting. She moved closer, stepping over crumbling stone and the tape keeping her out. It smelt of wet, decaying wood. Green moss grew up the jagged half-walls, thickly covering the grey stone that remained standing. She walked into the centre of what was left of the dwelling. Farther back she could see whole, sturdy structures, as if part of the castle had been reconstructed and restored back to its original state or perhaps it was still under construction. She noticed scaffolding adorning several different levels of what remained.

It was a massive space. Hannah turned in a full circle, concentrating on the dilapidated hallways that intersected the spot where she stood. Four separate corridors stretching north, south, east and west. The wind whistled down over the non-existent roof, following the open hallways like alleys. Hannah shivered at the eerie, forlorn sound it created. Some rotted shingle or loose plank somewhere off in the distance sustained a rhythmic, steady hammering.

She turned to face the breeze, letting it hit her fully in the face. What had she thought she would find here? Had she thought that Lock would just magically be here?

Hannah closed her eyes and inhaled deeply. The wind whipped around like a little tornado, pelting her with grit. "Oh, Lock," she breathed. She felt dizzy. Opening her eyes, she caught her balance and then caught her breath. She blinked rapidly, unable to believe her eyes.

She was standing in the centre of a finished gallery lined with art. Rich red runners lined the floors of each long hallway. Velvet ropes hung protecting the irreplaceable paintings from oily finger marks. She turned again in a circle, looking up at the still faces of the portraits. Generations of Munros stared back at her.

A gust swept grit and debris into her eyes. She yelped, trying to shield them. Her eyes watered furiously. She wiped them with the back of her hands in an attempt to clear the fragments, finally digging in the corners with her fingertips. Once cleared, blinking rapidly she realised the castle again lay in ruin.

She turned, bewildered. She began to cry. "I was here. It was finished. What happened to it? Your beautiful hall is in ruin. I don't understand," she wailed. Her voice seemed to carry in the vast emptiness bouncing off the rubble. She slumped down onto her knees. Covering her face, she sobbed. She hadn't taken any of the pills, hoping her mind would clear enough so that she could think without feeling like she was underwater. But she was even more confused now. "What's happening to me?"

* * * *

Llachlan swung viciously, levelling another wall. It was therapeutic. It was cathartic. Rebuilding Trafalis Hall to its original state was the only thing that kept him going. It gave him a reason to get up in the morning, to keep moving forward in his recovery. But today, it was keeping him from screaming at the top of his lungs. Frustration ate away at him.

Hannah. She hadn't called and it was driving him insane. Not knowing where she was disturbed him. And the thought that maybe he would never see her again clawed in his chest. He didn't know why this girl had got to him so deeply and so quickly. It was more than just a common bond. Something happened to him the minute she'd touched him. He'd felt alive. He'd felt territorial. He'd felt like dragging her by the hair into his cave like some Neanderthal and keeping her there.

Last night, when he'd finally crawled into bed—exhausted from the trip, then from spending half the evening reassuring his family that he was fine—she was all that he could think about. In his bed alone, he imagined again the desire he'd seen in those amazing eyes. He had played it over and over again in his mind, the moment when his fingers had grazed her zipper—and what he would have done if they'd been alone. He had thought about it until his cock was so rock hard he'd had to jerk off just to relieve the tension so that he could sleep. But even in sleep she wouldn't leave him any peace. She was there in his dreams, teasing him, challenging him to find her.

He swung the sledgehammer violently once again as his traitorous dick hardened even now, just thinking about her.

But the thought that plagued him, the one driving him, was that maybe it was her friend who was keeping her from calling him because she thought he was the one who had attacked her, just because his name was the same as the last person she thought she'd seen. Had she even been in Wales at the same time he was? And even if she had been, what were the odds that they could have even been in the same district? And what twist of fate would put them on the same plane to Glasgow to meet again?

It was impossible. But he honestly didn't know. It could have been him. Or whatever it was that drove him when he was not in control of himself during the lost time. He didn't think that he'd hurt anyone. But he couldn't be sure. He only remembered slivers of things—images, feelings, conversations—but never right away. They came to him in little snippets, like a dream that you'd forgotten you even had until something reminded you or triggered it. Just like yesterday, when he'd met Hannah and thought that he remembered her from another time—maybe even another woman—but there was something about her that was familiar.

It's Hannah and don't you forget it...

Where had that come from?

And the other bizarre thing was that she seemed to know him, too. So familiar, in fact, that she'd called him Llach. Only people close to him called him that. She'd looked into his eyes with confusion and sizzling hot desire. She'd been watching, waiting for something. But what? He threw the sledgehammer down in exasperation. And what of the portrait? How could she possibly know about that?

He leaned over and laid his hands on his thighs, trying to catch his breath, stretching out his sore back. He heard a strange sound. "What the hell is that now?" He listened.

It sounded like a woman. Crying. Things happened around the Hall all the time that made him think that the place might be haunted. He'd most likely go looking for the source and find nothing at all, then question his sanity yet again. The sound made his chest ache, so mournful. He wanted it to stop. It sounded like it was coming from the north end of the castle. He made his way in that direction and was surprised when the sound only got louder.

He stepped through the crumbling stone and into what someday he hoped would be the gallery to showcase all of the family portraits. A woman was crouched in the middle of the expanse, crying. He approached slowly, carefully, expecting the apparition to disappear. But as he closed in on her, his skin began to leap and charge with expectation. His heart pounded, his blood pumped.

"Hannah?" He knew that it was, even before she lifted her head.

Her head snapped up. "Lock?"

"Aye, lass, what are ya doin' here?" he asked, both baffled and exhilarated to see her.

She stood wiping at her eyes, blinking. "Llachlan?" she said again, in surprise.

He nodded, watching her.

"You're here." She shook her head as if bewildered that he would be. "What happened here?" she cried.

"What happened?" he questioned, shaking his head, not knowing what she was talking about.

"When I was here, the hall was beautiful."

Apprehension crawled coldly across the back of his neck. "When were ya here?"

"Last week," she sputtered.

"This part of the hall has looked this way for hundreds of years. I've only just finished restorin' parts of the back half of the castle. I've not started reconstruction up here as yet."

She shook her head, disorientated.

"I thought your friend said that you hadn't yet been to Scotland," he tried.

She closed her eyes and rubbed her temples. "But how could I know if I hadn't been here?"

He couldn't stand to see her this way. He knew what it was like to struggle. He took her into his arms. She didn't resist—in fact she came willingly, coiling her arms around his waist. His cock hardened immediately and surged. He closed his eyes and gritted his teeth. How was he supposed to comfort her when the only thing he wanted to do was fuck her? He'd never felt this way in his life. He had an overwhelming need to be with her. He didn't feel like himself. He was afraid that he was going to lose control. He didn't trust himself around her.

"I don't know," she whispered. "I don't know what's real. Nothing's real but you."

"And how am I ta know that you are real?" he asked, trying to keep the beast inside him from bursting free.

"I am as real as you are," she said, leaning back to look at him. She ran her thumb over his chin. The uncertainty in her eyes devastated him.

He pulled her back to him, placing his cheek next to hers, rubbing his unshaven jaw against her soft one. He felt so close to her. Inexplicably bound.

"What are ya doin' to me?" he pleaded. "I feel like I know ya, lass. I want nuthin' more than to kiss ya."

"Do it," she challenged him breathlessly.

Llach barely moved and his lips were on Hannah's. He closed his eyes when she opened to him immediately. He took control of her mouth. As soon as he did, flashes of her naked, writhing beneath him, blinded him behind his closed eyes. Glimpses of various beautiful body parts danced evocatively through his mind. Of her on top of him, kissing his chest. It was more than just wishing to see her like that. It was more like a memory.

Llachlan wrenched his mouth from hers. "Why do I know ya?" His chest heaved. "Why do I know that ya have a tattoo on the inside of your wrist?" His thumb stroked the soft skin there.

"The same reason that I know that you have one on your left bicep," she answered, also breathing hard. She wrapped her hands around his upper arms, holding him tightly as he tensed at her words. "You know me." She stared deeply into his eyes.

"How can I know that you have another just above your lovely left breast?" He imagined his lips closing over it and sucking softly, even though he could not remember exactly what the image depicted.

Hannah took hold of his chin. "Because you know me," she whispered, as her lips closed over his. She went wild in his arms, pressing her lovely little body against his hard one. She didn't kiss him timidly, like a guy expected a woman he'd just met to do. There was no exploration or awkwardness. She just went at him like a lover, driving him to forget to be gentle, driving the blackness in him to take over.

Her fingers battled with the clasp of his jeans as she palmed the length of his painful erection. He couldn't stifle the growl that erupted from his chest.

He snaked his hand down her stomach, heading for the destination that his hungry cock wanted to be. He thumbed the button open and slid down the nylon zipper. "And how do I know that when I reach down here you will be as smooth as silk?" He slid his hand into her panties and groaned loudly when he found exactly what he knew would be there. "Oh God, it feels beautiful." He slicked his fingers into the soft folds of her wonderfully wet cunt. He slipped a finger inside her. She gasped and clenched around him just as he'd known she would.

"I feel like I have already loved ya," he murmured against her temple. "Not like my excitement for ya is new, but that I have already sunk myself into your sweet heat and I canna wait to get back there."

She moaned and squirmed against his hand.

He licked his lips and groaned again. "How do I know how ya taste, lass?"

"You enjoy the taste of me." His cock jerked painfully at her words. "You said so."

A sharp pain sliced through his head. "I could walk around for eternity with the taste of you in my mouth, Hannah-lass," he said, but the thought was not his.

She captured his chin, looking straight into his eyes intensely, searching. "Lockhart?"

"Aye, Hannah-lass," he said, taking her lips savagely. He slammed her against the nearest half-wall and pushed her slacks to her ankles as she helped him shove his over his hips. His thick rod jutted impressively.

He used the wall for leverage, kneeing her legs apart, boosting her up by the hips. He fisted the head of his straining penis, guiding it to the entrance of her slick pussy. He held her up then practically dropped her onto his waiting shaft, impaling her. She screamed and the sound reverberated off the stone.

The minute he was buried in her scorching cunt, he thought of nothing but the ease with which he could move inside her, the velvet glide of least resistance that only bare flesh meeting bare flesh could produce.

His blood pounded in his ears as he mindlessly withdrew and thrust over and over. She drove every thought from his mind except for one. *Fuck!*

Every time he rammed into her, she made the most erotic little hiccup he'd ever heard, like he was expelling the very breath from her with every powerful plunge, followed by his own grunt of ecstasy. The sound of their loving echoed off the neglected stones of Trafalis, resonating in his feverishly blank mind, driving him ever faster until suddenly he shuddered, exploding hot cum inside her.

Llachlan slowly became aware of his surroundings as wind whipped around them. He eased her legs down from where he'd wrapped them around his hips so that he could have better access. Hannah trembled in his arms as his cock slipped out of her. "Did I hurt ya?" he breathed, knowing that he had—he'd been delirious with need. Brutal. He'd been aware of what he was doing the whole time. It was not like the other times that he couldn't remember what he was doing or saying. This time he had been present but driven by some inexplicable force coupled with his own need and craving for her, unable to stop himself. He'd wanted to claim her. Brand her so that every other man would know that she was his. As if loving her like a thoughtless, mindless animal somehow made sense?

She shook her head in answer to his question.

"Do not lie ta me," he said, tucking a finger under her chin, forcing her to look up at him. She breathed heavily through her mouth. Her eyes were wet and the sight made his chest hurt. "I'm sorry, Hannah. I didn't mean ta hurt you."

It all of a sudden felt wrong to him for them to be standing in the stones so utterly exposed. He stooped, reaching for her capris first, then pulled his own trousers back into place. He turned, perhaps foolishly putting his back to her, and adjusted himself, zipping up shakily.

Llachlan took a deep breath before turning to face Hannah. Her clothes were back in place, if not a little rumpled. She looked up at him. "Don't be sorry," she said, moving back into his arms. "You didn't do anything that I didn't want you to."

He closed his eyes and wrapped his strong arms around her, overwhelmed by feelings for this woman he'd just met and brutalised. His knees threatened to buckle with the intensity.

"I thought ya would get in touch with me, call me," he said tightly. "What possessed ya to drive all the way out here? I could have come to you."

"I didn't know that you'd be here. I had to see it for myself. I needed to know if I'd been here or not. Whether it was all just a dream. I thought maybe if I came here and saw it that it would trigger something."

"And ya believe you've been here but it was somehow different?"

"Yes." She pulled away and looked around. "It was done, it was completed. It was exquisite—all the portraits so beautifully done and displayed in chronological order in this vast gallery. Red runners stretched out down all four corridors in a big cross. And the velvet ropes kept the visitors from touching the precious paintings." She stared as if she were actually seeing them and the hair on the back of his neck stood up again. She described it exactly as he envisioned it in its completed state, in his own mind. It was his own plan, including opening it up to the public maybe to help offset the massive cost of this little venture and to share the exquisiteness of the portraits that depicted his family and their history.

"But you say it has been this way for hundreds of years," she continued. "So how could I have seen it that way?" She looked to him, uncertainty clouding her eyes.

"Well, let's say ya were here." That was the one thing he hated when he tried to explain something that he didn't understand and didn't remember to his own family. They scoffed at him, telling him it had never happened, and it just frustrated him all the more. "What were ya doin' here? What brought you to Trafalis Hall?"

Her brow dove and she bit her lip. "I was bringing something here."

"What?"

"A portrait," she stated, then waited for his response.

"Oh? Do ya remember which one?"

"Yes. The very same one that you went to Wales to acquire for your collection."

His eye twitched as he watched her. He nodded slowly.

"Didn't you wonder how I knew that you'd obtained it in Wales? Didn't you question how I knew his name?"

"Whose name?" He wanted to hear her say it.

"Lockhart Munro," she spoke his name and it echoed. Something inside him tightened. "You don't believe me," she said.

"No, I'm not sayin' I don't believe you. The point is that you believe it."

"But that's not enough. I hate this! I hate that I can't process what's fact from fiction. May I see it?" she asked quickly, her green eyes wide and desperate. He blinked, trying to keep up with her.

For some reason he didn't want to show her. He felt something similar to resentment for a moment and then brushed it away. "Sure, it's in the finished part of the castle." He reached for her hand. "This way." She placed her hand in his without hesitation. It felt right. Like it belonged there.

He guided her through the rubble of the old part of the castle and into the new part.

"Oh!" she breathed. "Have you done this all yourself?"

"Mostly. I've had some help, mainly since the accident. My family didn't want me working here alone."

"It's beautiful. Do you know what it looked like before?"

He had a vision in his mind. "No. I've just tried to make it look the way I think it would have. I've done some research of the time period."

"You've done a remarkable job." Her praise made him feel good.

He took her into the portrait room, where he had a vast majority of the collection amassed. Some others remained at his parents' house. She looked up at the portrait of him.

She smiled. "No sword for you, Llach?"

He wondered at that. "No, a mallet is my weapon of choice."

She chuckled and his stomach knotted.

She looked around. "Where is the portrait of Malcolm?"

He stopped cold. He'd never mentioned Malcolm to her by name. He was sure of it. He knew that he'd referred to his brother, but that was all.

"It's behind mine," he said slowly. "Why?"

"Why is it you got the mallet and he got to pose on the polo pony?"

"Because he actually plays polo. I do not."

She nodded to his explanation.

"Where did ya see our portraits, Hannah?"

"Here in the" — her face dropped — "gallery," she finished. "Oh, my God!" She gulped. "We've done this before. Just not quite here. It was there." She pointed to where they'd just come from. "Oh, my God! You were here!" She clutched her stomach, stumbling backward. Llachlan reached quickly to steady her. She covered her mouth and looked up at him with stunned wide eyes. She blinked rapidly. "Oh, my God!" she repeated, through her hand.

"Start again, Hannah."

"We brought the portrait here. And when I walked in there was no one around but I could hear what sounded like hammering from way off in the distance, just like I did today."

"If ya'd been here, I would have been workin'. I'm here almost every day."

"I yelled and you came." Her eyes searched his. "I thought you were him at first…"

"Who?"

"Lockhart."

His brows rose. His throat was suddenly dry. He swallowed hard before he spoke. "Ya thought I was Lockhart?"

"Yes, you look a lot like him, but then you weren't." She shook her head then went on quickly, "I told you that I had the portrait, and… Oh, oh!" she said and her eyes lit as she remembered some other detail. "I had it outside in a rented van. I told Cassie I rented a van.

She didn't believe me but I did. We needed it to transport the portrait."

"You keep sayin' 'we'. *We* needed it to transport and *we* brought the portrait. Who were ya with?"

She turned away from him.

"Who do ya think ya were with, Hannah?"

She continued keeping her back to him.

He took her by the arm. "I know better than anyone what it's like. You are safe with me. There is nuthin' that you can tell me that is goin' to shock me. After the things that I've been told that I've done and said since the accident, I promise ya I will not think you're crazy. You can tell me, and then maybe we can figure out your lost time, even if I can't remember my own."

She turned and looked into his eyes. "It was Lockhart. I was with Lockhart."

He nodded once slowly. "How is that possible?"

She swallowed. "He stepped out of the portrait."

He nodded again, his mind slowing. "A...ghost then?"

"You told me when I was here that you knew about the curse. That it was legend here at Trafalis."

"I did? I am not aware of any curse."

"May I see? Will you show him to me?"

She seemed attached to the portrait...to Lockhart. She didn't say 'will you show me *it*' but 'will you show me *him*'.

"It's right over there." He pointed to a dark corner where he'd propped it up and left it. He cocked the shade of the adjustable lamp on his draftsman's desk so that it illuminated the painting.

She stepped closer. She shook her head slightly, looked at him then back at the painting. "No..." she cried. "No..." Her eyes filled. "That's not him! That is not Lockhart! It's just like Jake. Jake wasn't Jake, and now Lockhart..."

Llachlan tried to gather her into his arms. She batted at him, unwilling to accept his comfort. "No... No, don't." She swung her arms away from him.

"No! Why does this keep happening? *You!*" she accused, pointing in his face. "*You* look more like him than *that* does!" She gestured towards it. "Why is that? Why are you him? Why am I attracted to you? Why do you say things to me that he said to me? Why when I look in your eyes do I see him?" she yelled.

He remembered vaguely when he was brutally fucking her among the stones she'd said his name. Not Llachlan but Lockhart. His gut tightened again when he realised he'd answered to it.

"Wait, wait, wait." His mind screeched to a halt. "Do you think you...had a...relationship with this...this apparition?"

"Yeah, yeah, I think I did," she said, defensively, as if challenging him to prove her wrong. "I know I did." She pulled her top down and showed him the fading fingerprints on her skin. "He did this to me! And he fucks just like you do! All male aggression and no technique!" she spat.

Llachlan opened his mouth then closed it again. He needed to think about that one. He'd never been accused of being a bad lover. But, then again, he'd only been after one thing out there with her. He'd just wanted to bury himself in her. He still wanted to. His cock jerked again at the thought.

He moved towards her and put his hands up.

"What are you doing?" she asked, eyeing him warily.

"Just let me check out a theory." He placed his hands very gently over her breasts, aligning his own fingertips with the prints on her skin. They matched perfectly.

She looked up at him her mouth open, her head tilted slightly to the side, her eyes huge pools of watery green. "Are you him?" she asked, confused and clearly on the verge of tears.

Llachlan inhaled deeply and removed his hands from her. Coldness crept across his shoulders in dread. "May I ask ya a personal question?" At her nod he asked, "When ya were attacked — were ya raped?" He was afraid of the answer. Could that be why he knew such intimate details about her body? Had he been the one who'd assaulted her outside the pub in Wales? Why he'd woken in the alley not knowing where he was or how he'd ended up there? And why hadn't he thought about that before he'd treated her so roughly outside? He scraped a hand down his unshaven cheek.

"No. I wasn't. Why do you ask me that?"

"I cannot think of any other reason why you would have my finger marks on you unless I was the one who mugged you in Wales."

"You didn't hurt me. Lockhart did this. I was not mugged. I was at the farmhouse in Wales with Jake and his gran finding the portrait," she rushed.

He cupped his hand over his eyes then dug his fingers brutally into his forehead.

"Did you have lost time when you were in Wales?" she asked him, softly.

He nodded.

"And you thought that you hurt me?"

He nodded again.

She looped her arms around his waist. "You didn't. I know it. Just like I know that he would never harm me." She looked over at the portrait. "But he is not him anymore." She pointed at the picture. "I know that you would never injure me."

"I don't know what I do when I am in a blackout. I just wake up and I am not where I was last."

"That's what happened to me. I was here, with the portrait and you, and then I woke up in the hospital and Cassie was telling me this cockamamie story about being jumped outside the bar."

"You cannot trust that it was not me. Because *I* brought the portrait here from Wales. Not you."

She released her hold on him and took a step back. She hung her head. "Then how do I know the things that I know? How do you know the things that you know?" They stared at one another for a moment, neither of them having any answers. "I think I should go," Hannah said.

He experienced that horrible feeling of abandonment again, just as he had on the plane. He didn't want her to leave him.

"Don't leave," he said, taking her hand.

She looked up at him searching his eyes. "Why? There is no rational reason that I should be here. I should just go home like Cassie said and leave this all behind me."

"No, don't go. Don't leave me."

"Why?" she asked again loudly, demanding.

He opened his mouth and spoke not the words that he intended. "Because you said that if you ever met a man like me ya would never leave."

Her eyes filled. "Llach-lan," she said his name slowly, pointedly and deliberately. "How did you know that Lockhart said that to me if he is not inside you or somehow a part of you? I don't even know how to explain? Do you have his memories?" she cried. "How can you know these things if you are not him?" she demanded, frantically.

"I don't know why I said that."

"Other than what just happened out there between you and I, you have not known me. How could you know the intimate things that you do about me if we hadn't already been together? I was not with that man in that portrait. I was with you. But you were different and when I came here and saw you with the portrait, and Trafalis was whole and complete, you didn't know me. *Again!*"

She was getting to the point of near hysteria and he wasn't far behind. What the fuck was going on?

"Let's go somewhere. And we'll talk. We'll just lay it all out, like a puzzle," he suggested. He stretched out his hand to her, and without hesitation, she placed hers in his.

Chapter Fourteen

Llachlan led Hannah deeper into the castle, to the part that he lived in for now. It was just one huge room, really, with a living space, a kitchenette, a bathroom and his bed. He'd worked long hours here and sometimes just crashed whenever he grew too tired to do any more. He'd wake up, eat and start again. Finishing Trafalis Hall was like an obsession to him. At least, before Hannah it had been.

She smiled softly. "It looks so out of place here," she said, looking. "Such a modern room, in such a romantic, medieval setting. It's like it doesn't belong."

"It's how I feel in life now," he said, running water into the kettle. "Like I don't belong, even in my own family. It's so strained. They tiptoe around me like I might crack, or they look at me like I now own three heads when I speak."

She looked out the window, down to the stones below. "You are lucky, though. You have family. They obviously love you. They'll stand by you and get you through this."

"Have you no one? Besides your friend Cassie?"

She shook her head but didn't elaborate.

"You will have me," he said, looking at the back of her head.

She nodded slightly. "For now. While I'm here. But at some point, I will have to return home. I only have two weeks left of vacation time."

His lips tightened as he tried to keep the roar inside him from coming out. If it was the last thing he did, she would not return home.

"But you know, Llach, I think we both need to accept that we are different now—that things are never going to go back to what they were before. Maybe the sooner we do, the better off we'll be. Maybe your family needs to accept that as well. They're not going to get back the Llachlan that they remember, but that's okay because you are alive and things will get better. Things won't always be like this—they'll just be different and maybe even better, who knows?"

He moved in behind her and slid his hands down her arms, then pulled her back against him. "You make me feel good," he whispered near her ear. "Like there is hope. Nothing has made me feel that way since the accident."

She turned in his arms and placed hers around his neck. "And I have never felt anything like what I feel for you."

"You mean Lockhart," he corrected, his stomach twisting again at the thought of her feeling these things for someone else.

"I'm not sure that I do mean Lockhart." Her eyes delved deeply into his. She made him hard just looking at him like that. As soon as she felt his hard cock digging into her, her eyes softened.

"Come, sit down and tell me everything that you remember," he said, not giving in to the desire. They'd never get any of this sorted out if he did. She seemed to think the same.

She sat on a stool at the counter as he poured the boiling water for tea. "I will. On one condition."

"What's that?"

"First you tell me what caused your accident."

"Not much to tell really." He sat on a stool facing her. "I was here workin' on the castle and a board from the scaffold blew down and bashed me in the head. Malcolm found me hours later when he couldn't reach me on my cell."

"Were you working outside?"

"No. I was in the room that we just left. The one temporarily housin' the portraits."

She swallowed as something danced in her head just out of her reach. "You said it blew down. Did the wind come up?"

"I meant it fell," he rushed. "It fell down. Of course, the wind couldn't come up inside."

"So what happened when your brother found you?"

"He said there was a lot of blood and he thought I was dead when he first saw me. He checked for a pulse and then called for help. I spent the next week, so they tell me, in a coma."

"Do you remember anything?"

"Just bits and pieces. Nothing concrete." Nothing that made sense or that he was willing to share with anybody else. They were just too ludicrous to say out loud. "Then they gave me a bunch of pills to take, and, well, you know about that, right?"

She nodded. "They make you feel like you're not really in the moment."

"So, tell me what you remember."

"I travelled from Canada to London, spent a week in London sightseeing then I travelled to Wales. Now, what version would you like to hear from then on? The one Cassie would like me to believe, or the one I would like to…"

"Re-live?" he supplied.

She looked away.

"You said when I first met you that you lived more in those three days than you had your whole life and you wished to repeat them over and over. What is it Lockhart did for you that made you feel the need to duplicate them indefinitely?"

She blushed. "He loved me," she said softly.

Llachlan felt like he'd been slugged in the stomach. "And what made his lovin' so grand?"

"No, he said he loved me."

"I find it hard ta believe that you've not heard that particular endearment before." She was beautiful. There was not a chance in hell that dozens of guys hadn't said those words to her.

"I've heard it before. But I never believed it until he said it."

"So ya arrived in Wales, then what?" he asked, not wanting to hear what another man had said to her and made her believe.

"I missed the last bus to Swansea and the bus station closed. The next one didn't run until ten the next morning. Jake had been on the bus with me and was catching a ride the rest of the way to his house. When he saw that I was standing outside by myself, he and his gran pulled up and they offered to take me to Swansea. At first I didn't want to accept but he said they couldn't leave me there. I looked down the street at the pub and, well…I didn't think I should stay there, either. But as we got driving, it was a nasty night—a real storm—wind, thunder and lightning. We were stopped by a policeman who told Gran to turn around and just return home—that they were advising everyone to stay off the roads. So they took me back to their farmhouse. But when we drove up, lightning flashed and I saw the farmhouse as a castle."

"A castle."

"Well, to be honest what I saw was Trafalis Hall, but I didn't know that until I came here and saw it—not the way it sits now but the way it should look when it's completed...or was completed, or..." She shook her head. "Anyway, when I got inside at Jake's, I wasn't feeling well and I went up to my room. I kept feeling dizzy and seeing shadows and that's when I noticed the portrait of Lockhart. But not the one that you have. As I said, the Lockhart portrait that I saw looked just like you. Except for the one little dimple that you have that he didn't, everything else about you was the same. The dark hair and eyes, the cleft in the chin, the accent, the swagger, the attraction, the pull."

"The pull?"

"Yes, every time I neared the portrait or him, I felt like I was being drawn towards him."

"And ya feel that with me?"

"Yes, do you not...feel it?" Her eyes looked worried.

"Aye, I do," he admitted, nodding slightly.

She looked somewhat relieved. "At first, I just stared at the portrait. It intrigued me. It was so lifelike and in the firelight of the room, it was like he was moving. I just thought I was feverish. I went to sleep and when I woke up my throat hurt, so I went down to the kitchen to find some juice and he was there."

"He was there? But not as a portrait?"

"No, he was a man. Flesh and blood."

"Did he scare you?"

"I was a little startled but as I said, intrigued. You are an exceedingly handsome man, you know—it is extremely hard not to be fascinated."

"It wasn't me, it was a... I don't even know, and we'll talk about what's extremely hard later." She smiled at the joke. "Continue, what happened then?"

She scratched the back of her head absent-mindedly and would not look at him. "We, uh, went back upstairs."

"You took a strange man back to your room?"

"Don't be so shocked. It's not like I've ever done such a thing before, and may I remind you that I am a stranger to you and we just did it outside in the daylight where anyone could have seen us? You didn't seem outraged then."

"So what? Ya had sex with him. Then what?"

"When I woke up in the morning he was gone, and when I asked Jake about him, Jake said that if I'd in fact run into the guy from the portrait then I had run into a ghost. So I hightailed it out of there as fast as I could, trying to convince myself that I'd been sick and feverish and that I'd dreamt the whole freakin' debacle."

"But you had real feeling for it."

"For him, yes."

"Where did you go?"

"I hopped the ten a.m. bus going to Swansea. But he appeared to me on the bus."

Llachlan's eyes widened.

"I tried to tell him to go away, that he wasn't real, but—get this—he was pissed off at me for leaving."

Something tickled at the back of Llachlan's mind and he said the words that were not his own, just as he had in the portrait room. "Because you said that if you ever met a man like me ya would never leave."

She nodded. "How do you know that?" she challenged him to explain.

"I don't know," he dismissed. "Go on."

"He said the pull from the portrait was strong. I told him to drop dead and he said, 'You're about four hundred years too late', then he disappeared. I went to my hotel room and he appeared to me again. That's when he told me that he needed my help. That he had been cursed into the painting and he needed me to return the portrait to his home to break the curse."

"Trafalis Hall."

"Yes, so I went back to Jake and Gran's, purchased the painting, rented a van and he and I started towards Airdrie to bring him home."

"And?"

"We stopped once so that I could rest. And he…" she sighed.

"He what?"

"He told me that he loved me, and he went back into the painting and never came back out. I wasn't sure if that had broken the curse or not, but I had promised that I would take him home and that's what I did. I brought the portrait to Trafalis. But not this Trafalis. The finished one. I told you, I came in, I heard the hammering. I hollered hello several times, then you came out and I thought that you were him. And then things kind of get fuzzy. But I've remembered a lot just saying it all out loud."

"Take your time, then, it'll come." He poured her a cup of tea and one for himself. She took a sip.

"I took you outside to see the portrait, but it had aged and weathered somehow overnight and was almost unrecognisable. But you said you might be able to restore it. We came back inside and you showed me your portrait, leaning on the mallet. Malcolm's was alongside yours and then beside that was a wedding portrait of your mum and dad. Your Dad's name is…um…" She tapped her index finger on her upper lip as she thought. "Okay, I can't recall your dad's right now, but don't tell me—I want to remember on my own. Your mother's name is…Muirial." Her eyes sought his for confirmation.

He nodded as another cold shudder passed through him.

"How would I know that?"

"I don't know. 'Tis common knowledge, I assume."

"For a crazy Canadian tourist that has never even heard of you?"

"Go on. Where did I take you next?"

"I want to remember your dad's name first."

"Continue, it will come or it won't."

"You took me down the west corridor—you said it was where the 'ancient ones' were. I remember thinking that Lockhart didn't seem ancient to me and I resented you saying that about him." She looked at him accusingly.

"Do you want me to apologise for somethin' I did not say?"

"No, of course not. Your dad's name is Kerr."

His only acknowledgement was a blink of his eyes and the tightening of his jaw.

"You showed me a painting of Llachlan Munro, Lockhart's father. You said that is who you were named after. Is that true?"

He pursed his lips in confirmation.

"Next to that was a portrait of Lockhart's mum, Eveolyn. Correct?"

"Aye."

"Next to that was a portrait of Lockhart, an exact replica of the one that I brought. You told me that Lockhart's father had one painted just like the one that went missing. And next to that one was a portrayal of what Lockhart might have looked like if he'd aged."

"If he'd aged?"

"Yes, you explained that, in his declining years, Lock's father had a portrait done of what his son may have looked like if he'd…not disappeared."

"What did they think happened to him?"

"Well, some believed he deserted, because the day after he disappeared he was supposed to report to take up his commission. But you also told me that his father did not believe this story and he made it his life's work to find out what happened to his son. He documented everything that he learned about the curse and he made sure that it was handed down through the generations. Do you have these documents?"

Llachlan shrugged. "I have never heard of this. So explain to me this curse."

She took her time trying to remember. "It was the artist who painted the portrait. She fell in love with Lock but he did not return her feelings, although he did admit to me that he may have had his fun with her…"

"The artist was female? Is that not rare back in those days?"

"Yes. I'm trying to remember her name. She was a MacAllister."

A visible shudder shook Llach's body.

"Some things never change. You told me MacAllisters were banned from Trafalis. What was her name? Started with an L—Lil, Lillian…"

"Lillias," he said.

"Yes, yes, that's it! You know of her?"

"Yes, she is in the family tree. She is Lockhart's wife."

"*What*?" Hannah paled.

"Aye. Some of what you say rings true. As the stories go, the night before Lockhart was to leave to take up his commission, he had more than his fun with her and it resulted in a child. He was forced to return home to marry her at his father's insistence. It was not a love match. Their battles were legendary. She finally ended it by throwing herself from—"

"His chamber window," Hannah finished.

"Yes. She did this in your, uh, adaptation as well?"

"When Lock would not return her love, she went to a witch, also a MacAllister, and they poisoned him with some kind of tainted wine. He was paralysed. They chanted some kind of spell while burning herbs and such. Lock said his body was transported into the portrait. He said Lillias tempted him and taunted him, but he was so angry with her for what she'd brought upon him, he would never return her love. When she realised it was a lost cause, she threw herself over. He watched from inside the painting. There was nothing he could do. The witch who'd helped Lillias with the curse had the painting stolen and sent to Wales. In time, Lock's father tracked the witch down and she told him all he would need to get his son back. She told him everything except where the painting was. Without it, there was no Lockhart. He told me that while he was here at Trafalis, he was unable to move outside of the portrait, but once he found himself in Wales, he discovered ways to come out."

"What did this curse entail?"

"I'm not sure that even Lock was positive of the whole of it. He said to break the curse he needed to return Lillias' love, which he couldn't do because he was so angry with her for what she'd done to him, and she needed to love unselfishly and let him go — allow him to serve."

"So when he told you he loved you, you think that may have broken the spell?"

"I hope he is free. It's what he wanted — what he needed after all that time and desolation."

"Now tell me Cassie's version of what happened to you."

"I got off the bus in Wales, some drunks from the bar roughed me up and I woke up in the hospital."

"Did you remember any of this when you first woke up?"

"I just knew that you were gone — that he was gone. I just felt this deep emptiness without...him. But as time went on, I remembered what I thought was true, then they brought Jake to see me and he was not the Jake that I remembered. And now the portrait of Lockhart is not what I saw either. It's like two totally different realities with many common threads."

"But dreams are that way, are they not? They are always things that are somewhat familiar to us, just different," Llachlan said.

"I thought you said the point was that *I* believed it was real."

"I believe you believe it was real." Her lips thinned at his uncertainty. "But I will admit you know details about things that you probably shouldn't know. And I have no explanation for that," he allowed.

"Just as you have no explanation as to why you can repeat word for word things that Lockhart said to me. You know intimate details about me that you shouldn't."

"I have explained that. And I'm afraid that I hurt you, and even more terrified that I might harm you again because when I am with you I feel quite...out of control."

"That's him. I know it is. He has no control and if he is acting through you…"

She stopped speaking when he started to rub his eyes. "Maybe this is enough for now. I should go," she said again.

"*No!* Don't go." His voice sounded overloud and discordant, not at all like him.

She looked at him. "See! Was that you?"

He exhaled angrily. "Of course, it was. I'm afraid you are goin' to be disappointed when you realise that he is not here. He is not in me. This thing that is happenin' is happenin' between you and me, not you and him. This is just me. And I may not be altogether sane."

"Well, then we have a club, don't we? Because I'm not feeling altogether sane myself. But I need to leave. Whatever is happening or not happening will have to wait. Cassie will be sending out a search party for me any minute."

"Call her," he said, desperately. "Let her know that you're okay. You are fine here," he tried to reassure her. "Stay with me." His dark eyes searched hers. "Please." He moved closer to her, his face just inches from hers. "Besides, ya owe me another chance," he said, his eyes warming.

"Another chance?"

"Aye, 'all male aggression and no technique'? You must allow me to redeem myself. All male aggression, I may be, but I will prove to ya that I have great technique and it just may take me all night long to demonstrate." He leaned in and touched his lips to hers. "Call her. Tell her not to wait up," he finished, his dark eyes full of smouldering promise.

Hannah scrambled to call Cassie, hitting the quick dial.

"*Hello,*" Cassie snapped.

"Hey, Cass—"

"Where the fuck are you?"

Hannah exchanged a look with Llach, knowing that he could hear the tirade on the other end.

"I'm fine. Okay? I just wanted to let you know…"

Llachlan slid a finger slowly over Hannah's bottom lip, over her chin, tracing the column of her throat, finally stroking the valley between her breasts. She straightened her shoulders, thrusting her chest out for him.

"Damn it, Hannah—seriously, tell me where you are. I am coming to get you."

"No. Listen to me. I'm fine. I just needed to have some time to myself and sort some things out. I'll call you tomorrow…"

Llachlan undid the top button of her blouse, then the second, and third, keeping his dark eyes on hers the whole time. When her blouse was open, he skimmed his warm palms around her slim waist, then around to her back where he massaged her hips robustly. It almost hurt, his strong hands not knowing their own strength. But she liked it.

"Tomorrow! Are you out of your mind?" Cassie screeched. "Oh, look who I'm talking to. Yes, you *are* out of your mind! I did not come all this way just to chase you all over this country, spending my time alone!"

"Well, now you'll know how I felt when you bailed on me."

"Oh, this is so totally different and you know it!"

Hannah pulled the phone away from her ear and looked at Llach sheepishly. He took the phone and placed it on the counter. Llachlan skimmed his hands into her blouse and coaxed it from her shoulders. He undid the clasp on her capris, taking the zipper down, then eased the pants from her hips, letting them glide down her legs. She stood in front of him in only a mauve-coloured bra and panties. She vaguely heard Cassie's shrill voice on the phone.

Llachlan backed away from her slightly, letting his gaze run all the way down her body then back up as if he'd never seen her before. When his eyes finally met hers, she inhaled sharply at the raw desire she saw reflected back at her. He covered his chest with one large hand, while shaking his head and blowing out a deep breath through his lips in appreciation. "*Wow!*" he mouthed.

"*Hannah!* Damn it, Hannah, answer me!"

"Oh shit, Cassie!" Hannah pulled the phone back to her ear.

Llachlan leaned in and pressed another kiss to her lips. "I'll be in the shower," he said with a slight side motion of his head in the direction of the bathroom.

"Who was that? Are you with him? Is that where you are? I'll find that fuckin' card and I will come and get you."

Llachlan undid the top button of his jeans and slid the zipper down while backing his way towards the bathroom. Hannah swallowed hard when his jeans gaped at the waist, exposing his cut hips, giving her the impression that the denim could fall at any moment. She tried to will it with her mind. She wondered what was holding them up when her gaze travelled lower to the impressive bulge straining temptingly against his shorts.

"Hannah! Are you even listening to me?"

"Yeah," she answered weakly, her mouth suddenly dry.

He made it to the bathroom door then reached behind his head with one hand to pull the neck of his tight-fitting T-shirt over his head, ruffling his dark hair, making Hannah's fingers itch to smooth it down. He dragged the shirt the rest of the way down his arms and bared his powerfully built chest. He was even more sculpted than she remembered, most likely from all the construction. He tossed the tee in her direction and grinned cockily at the look on her face, bringing out the dimple in his cheek.

"Tell me where you are. I just looked in my purse and that card is gone, Hannah. Give me the address. Now!"

Llachlan turned and pushed his jeans down over his hips, giving her the full view of his toned ass before he disappeared, leaving the door invitingly ajar. Hannah heard the spray of water.

"Cass, I gotta go!" she said. After quickly ending the call, she sprinted for the open door.

Chapter Fifteen

Hannah entered the bathroom. The shower was in the corner.

It was open-plan, without doors, lined in terracotta tile. A huge showerhead sprouted from the centre of the stall, raining a waterfall over his glorious body. He stood under the spout with his face raised to the spray — his feet slightly spread apart, supporting his muscular thighs, his impressive hard-on jutting out proudly.

"Are ya going to stand there watchin' or will ya join me, Hannah-lass?" he asked, running his hands through his wet hair and stepping back out of the water so that he could see her.

She wondered if he was even aware that he was calling her that. It was what Lockhart had called her.

A little bit of the devil crept into her and she thought to have some fun with him. "I just came in to tell you that Cass is on her way to pick me up." She even turned in the direction of the door, giving the impression she was leaving. "So, I'll be seeing you…"

Hannah didn't get to finish when Llach slammed into her, his hard wet chest against her back. He embraced her, stopping her progress.

Hannah laughed as breath rushed from her lungs at the impact.

"I don't think so," he said, his voice deep and insistent. "Not unless she wants to get an eyeful. Because you are not leavin' here until I'm good and done with ya." His salacious promises coupled with the seductive accent sent goosebumps skittering over her skin.

She turned in his arms and threw hers around his neck, stretching to reach his searching mouth. As he kissed her, he dragged her backward into the shower.

"I'm still half dressed!" she exclaimed, as he pulled her under the spray.

"Ya won't need your clothes," he said into her mouth, the water making their lips slippery, giving them an extra sensual glide.

He leaned over and turned a knob, changing the water from a spray to a warm mist, then he flicked another switch, making the stall glow with a red hue. She immediately felt warmth beaming down on her shoulders.

She smiled into his lips. "Heat lamps—really?"

"Aye, infrared. Every old castle should be equipped, don't ya think?"

"Of course, only the best."

"Aye, only the best," he purred. He worked his arms behind her back, undoing the hooks of her bra, moving to coax it from her. His pupils dilated as he stared down at her bared flesh.

She moved back into his embrace, swishing her full breasts over his wet chest. Her nipples puckered at the sensation, the fine mist of water making them slide over his skin effortlessly. An appreciative hum reverberated through his chest.

Llachlan dropped to his knees. Following the line of her bikini-cut panties, he ran his lips slowly along her stomach. Her tummy clenched with excitement and anticipation. He flicked his wet, warm tongue quickly across her skin just inside the elastic. He brushed his hands slowly up her calves, teasing her thighs. Her leg muscles quivered under his touch. Tucking his index fingers into the thin elastic creasing her hips, he dragged the scrap of lace down her legs. Hannah looked down at the top of Llachlan's dark head as he stared at her smooth mound. He groaned, his hot breath exhaling in a rush, hitting her thighs, causing another round of sensation to erupt all over her body.

Llachlan laid a soft kiss on her flesh just above her hidden clit, where she longed for his caress. He firmly clamped his large, warm hands around her backside, holding her.

He smoothed his open lips across her wet skin, the warm drizzle from the shower coating everything in fine moisture. He kissed her again, this time sliding his tongue into her slit, setting every sensitive nerve ending she owned on pulse.

"Mmm," he hummed, as if savouring her taste. "Sweet honey."

Does he remember? she thought distractedly. It was what Lock had said back at the farmhouse, she realised, but she didn't bring it to his attention, not wanting to sidetrack him. Hannah stroked her fingers along his jaw line, holding him to her, encouraging him forward. His tongue stroked over her softly, tasting then retreating as if he had all the time in the world. He opened her a little more with every velvety stroke, only to withdraw again. Her pussy swelled with heavy need for him to plunge something into her, anything—needing him to fill the emptiness. She was almost begging for him to end the sweet torture. He had her on the thin edge, teasing then retracting, using only the feathery lush sweep of his masterful tongue, as if she were the most delicate of subjects. Hannah began to squirm, rising up onto her tiptoes, thrusting her pelvis forward, offering herself up to him.

The tension in her built as he ran his fingers through the slickness, spreading it around the smooth folds, while gently tapping her clit with the flat of his tongue.

"Ahh," Hannah moaned. "I don't want to come yet!" she cried, fisting her hands into his hair, her toes curling into the hard tile in an attempt to prolong the sweet suffering.

She felt his lips curve into a grin against her skin. "Come, Hannah-lass. 'Tis just the first of many this night. I promise. Let me feel your pleasure on my tongue." He fluttered the end of it, tickling the engorged nub.

Llachlan parted her lips with his thumbs, pulling back hard enough that the coiled little bud jutted out, exposing every raw nerve ending to the cool air as well as his skill. He barely grazed the delicate little button when her breath hissed between her teeth. It was as if he were being extra careful and gentle with her after the way they'd gone at it outside.

Hannah dug her fingers into his shoulders, holding onto him. Her clit felt like it was burning but cool at the same time. The pleasure was so raw—it almost hurt, but it was the most pleasurable pain.

He wiggled the end of his tongue so gently, barely even making contact. Every muscle she owned tightened, waiting. He took the sensitive bump between his lips and gave it the tiniest little suck. She let herself go with the promise of more.

Hannah's tightened her palms against his jaw as she stiffened and juddered, riding the waves of sumptuous bliss. A low moan escaped her dry throat as he released his thumbs from holding her open. He swirled his plundering tongue from her blazing clit to her spasming, hot hole, drawing out the exquisite climax for her. He mashed his face into her softness, giving her as much as he could.

Hannah was desperate now to feel him inside her. She needed him. She craved him. She wanted him to slam into her. She needed to feel the velvet glide of his cock pulsating and plunging, pushing her to forget all her doubts and delusions. She wanted him to fuck her, hard.

He stood from his kneeling position, facing her. His powerful chest heaved—his jaw was tight with obvious restraint. His dark eyes focused intensely on her and she knew he needed the same. Another wicked thrill stabbed through her as he wiped his hand down his face—the wetness, she knew, was not totally from the shower.

"Turn around," he all but snarled. Not waiting for her to comply, he twisted her around by the arms, placing her palms flat against the cool tile. He kept his hands over hers for a moment, instructing her silently to obey him and keep her hands there. "Hold on," his voice rasped in her ear. She felt his teeth graze the base of her neck, sending another buzz of sensation skittering over her wet skin. Then he parted her legs.

He rubbed his thick cock back and forth between her thighs. "Open," he demanded, parting the full curves of her ass. The roughness of his work-worn knuckles nudged her wet folds as he choked his swollen shaft and began to guide himself into her. She lifted up onto her tiptoes and thrust her rear end out to accommodate him.

Hannah felt the tip of his rigid cock nudge only an inch into her ravenous cunt. She began to bear down on him. She wanted all of him. She couldn't stand for him to work at this slow and delicate the way he'd licked her pussy. She moved her hands down the wall, planting them just as he rammed urgently forward, burying himself completely, driving deep. A hot, sharp spontaneous rush of searing heat stole her breath for a moment. She needed to move, her body clamouring to feel him pistoning inside her.

"Oh, God, ya feel so good," he growled. His fingers tightened on her hips. "Stay still," he pleaded. "I don't wanna come yet either," he admitted, his words tight through gritted teeth.

She looked invitingly over her shoulder at him, pushing her bum more fully against him. "The first of many tonight, Llach," she promised him raggedly.

He snarled when she tightened her inside muscles around him, encouraging him to give her what she wanted — what they both needed.

He retreated painstakingly slowly, then slammed home, causing her to cry out. He paused, withdrawing inch by painful inch only to ram his rock-hard erection fully into her.

"Faster," she demanded on a needy sob, shimmying her bottom against him.

Instead of doing as she demanded, he reached to his side and pumped the plunger on the soap dispenser, filling the air with his spicy masculine scent. She whimpered — irritated, so aroused and still being denied the sweet erotic glide of his cock plunging into her. He soaped the palms of his hands and slithered them slowly over her ass in circles, then dug in his thumbs almost too hard on either side of her spine, slowly tracing up her back, cupping over her shoulders, partway down her arms before slipping his hands over her breasts.

"You are too used to having your own way," his deep accent hummed in her ear as he leaned over her, his chest against her back. "You didn't want to come but ya are in a big hurry to get somewhere. Slow down and enjoy." He opened his hands and circled her erect nipples with his soapy palms, all the while keeping up a slow, erotic grind. She groaned at the titillating sensation he created, sending a shockwave of feeling from her tingling tits straight to the deep dark place inside her, making her pussy clench around him.

"Mmm," he groaned, in response. "Ya like that, don't ya, my Hannah-lass?"

"God, yes! You know I do! Please!" she begged.

"Please what?" he goaded. "Say it."

With maddening slowness, he stroked his fingers over her skin, finally plucking her nipples. Hannah was desperate for some release. Was he going to make her beg for it? She removed her hand from the wall and had every intention of taking matters into her own hands and stimulating her own clit when he seized her wrist. "You are not the only one who knows how to give you pleasure."

"Then do it! Give it to me!" she demanded, through clenched teeth. "You are driving me crazy!" she all but sobbed, a bundle of raw nerves quivering for his touch.

"You do the same to me. From the first time I laid eyes on you in the terminal, I had an instant hard-on. I could already see us together. Your beautiful flesh bared to me. Your amazing body crawling over my chest..."

"Because we've been like this before!" she snapped. She took his hands and spread them over her breasts, kneading his hands under hers just as she'd done with Lockhart. "Remember..." she implored, panting.

"Remove your hands," he instructed, firmly. She once more thought he was pissed off that she wanted to be in control.

She did as he asked. He waited until she'd moved before he stroked her foamy, slippery nipples until they burned with tingling energy, increasing the intolerable pressure inside her.

"It feels so good," she moaned, rocking her ass against him. His cock jerked inside her, starting the fluttery waves of a brilliant orgasm radiating from deep within her.

Her tight pussy started contracting, squeezing him from root to tip. She bent forward, pulling him even deeper into her scorching heat, sending his cock into its own trembling, pulsing peak. He roared, pushing her hips away from him, then pulling her back. He plunged and retreated in a frenzy, over and over, in mindless gratification. She made the same little spontaneous hiccup as she had outside, every time he slammed into her. He shuddered, finally squirting deep inside her.

He slowed his pace as they both struggled to catch their breath.

She stood straight from her bowed position — forcing him up with her, she cushioned her back against his chest. Bending slightly, he wound his arms around her. "Well, that was definitely worth the wait," she purred languidly, rubbing her slippery backside against him.

"I told ya," he chuckled, sounding quite full of himself.

She turned in his arms. "It's really not my fault that just looking at you turns me on," she said.

"I suppose that is my fault for bein' so damned irresistible?" he said, teasing her.

She looked up into his eyes. He was being playful, just like Lockhart. This Llachlan seemed so serious — for good reason, she supposed. Could she really differentiate between the two men, or were they one and the same? There were so many things that they did and said that made it seem like they were one. She wanted them both. The fun-loving, mischievous Lockhart wrapped up in the gloriously beautiful Llachlan package.

"What?" he asked, his eyes narrowing slightly in question.

"Nothing." She sloughed off the feeling. "Let's get cleaned up before we both look like prunes. Besides, it's hot in here," she said, looking up at the heat lamps as well as the steam.

He grinned. "Naw, that's just me."

She rolled her eyes and released her hold on him, reaching for the soap pump that he'd used earlier. She turned and rubbed the soap over his chest and arms, when her gaze landed on his tattoo. She inhaled in surprise.

"It's different!" she exclaimed, wiping the soap away from the dark symbol.

She traced the Celt design with her fingertip.

"What's different about it?" he asked carefully.

"The top is the same. Like a crude Celtic cross, but that's all his was. It was a cross. Yours morphs into...a key," she said in wonder.

"'Tis a Celtic Key," he explained.

She met his gaze again in complete confusion. "It's like he's half here." Her gaze drifted over his arm. "Do you remember getting it?"

"I don't recall getting it. As far as I know, I woke up with it after the accident. It looked foreign to me, on my own skin. I asked my brother Malcolm about it and he explained to me that he has the exact same tattoo. Apparently, it is a team tradition. All our mates on the rugby team got one when we won the playoffs."

She felt deep disappointment. It was just one more thing that couldn't be explained. She stared up at him, looking for the answers he couldn't give her.

He dropped a kiss on the end of her nose. "I have a beautiful, willing, naked woman in my shower. I'd rather not waste our time tryin' to figure this out."

He reached for a thick washcloth and hit the lever, making warm water stream down on them.

"I thought that was exactly what we were supposed to be doing. Isn't that why you gave me your card? So that we could help each other? Or are you just helping yourself?" she asked.

"Helpin' myself? I believe you are a willin' participant," he retorted.

"Yeah, and you didn't hear me complaining either, right?" she said, softly recalling Lock's words to her.

"What's that then? Somethin' else he said to ya that you think I should remember?" he said with some heat.

HK Carlton

She lowered her head avoiding his gaze. She caught her lip between her teeth trying to keep the tears that were threatening from falling.

"Maybe I *should* go," she mumbled, all of a sudden feeling as naked as she was. "This isn't helping either one of us." She attempted to move past him, but he would have none of it.

"Ya aren't goin' anywhere. Ya don't want to leave me, anymore than I want ya to leave," he said, tipping her head back. He devoured her lips.

"Do ya...want to leave?" he asked, coming up for air.

He turned his intense dark eyes on her. "No," she admitted softly. But she was afraid of getting in any deeper. She was beginning to get way too wound up with him. Far too invested, way too fast. Just as she'd done with Lockhart. As if she couldn't help herself. As if some other driving force was compelling her, perhaps even them, together. She was falling in love with them, with him. How could this be? She'd closed her heart. She couldn't allow herself to get hurt. She had to go back home at some point and continue her life. Didn't she? "But I'm afraid..."

"Not tonight." He brushed her wet hair back. "Neither one of us will worry about tomorrow until tomorrow."

He stared at her until she nodded in agreement. His face lightened, losing some of its tension.

"Now..." He handed her a washcloth. "You will wash me, woman." He grinned cockily. He placed his hands on his hips and splayed his feet wide in a warrior's stance. She grinned in spite of herself. That was a very Lockhart command and pose if she'd ever seen one.

Hannah pumped more soap into her hand and lathered it with the washcloth. She smoothed it over the back of his neck, stretching to reach him. He took hold of her, curving his palms around her slim waist. She dragged the soft rag over his powerful shoulders, down his bulging biceps, allowing her gaze to linger on the key on his arm, before she admired his upper body.

She sighed as she felt herself becoming warm again. The sight of him, the feel of his warm firm flesh under her hands, the smell of his soap swirling around them, made her want him all over again. He dropped his hips slightly and moved closer to her in an outwardly relaxed stance, but she felt his burgeoning erection bump against her. She circled the cloth lower, washing his muscled torso. A rough sound of appreciation reverberated through his chest.

She gathered up a handful of lather and moved on to the part of him that they both wanted her to touch. She cupped his sac with one firm hand while taking his lengthening cock in the other palm. She curved her thumb and fingers around the hardening shaft, taking a lazy, sensual journey up to the smooth head.

"Oh!" she gaped in surprise, her eyes darted to his. Llachlan was different from Lockhart. How could this be?

He returned her look, eyes heavy-lidded in arousal, enjoying her attention. He gave her a crooked grin, evidently mistaking her surprise for appreciation.

Llachlan was circumcised. How had she not noticed this before now? she wondered, massaging the smooth head of his jutting penis. She guessed because erect they didn't appear *that* much different. And Lockhart had almost always maintained an impressive hard-on. And this session with Llachlan, he'd been the aggressor and she'd just enjoyed him—not paying much attention to what was going on down there until now. It was like she'd been with two different men in the last week, but not. She tried to push it all to the back of her mind for now and just concentrate on the beautiful hunk of man that was in her hands right now.

Hannah stroked him expertly—long and slow at first, upping the tempo of the soapy, rhythmic tug until his breathing was rough and laboured. His hips began to thrust as he lost himself in the determined, unrelenting jerking of her hand.

"Oh God!" he rasped. "Ah, fuck!" he groaned, attempting to grab the end of his cock and seal his thumb over the opening before he came. Hannah kept a firm hold of him and he jetted hot semen across her stomach.

"Oh, fuck, I'm sorry," he panted, rushing to apologise. He pushed his shaft up against her stomach and looked down at her. His gaze lingered on the creamy cum streaked across her skin, making her wonder if he found it as weirdly satisfying as she had earlier when he'd wiped her wetness from his face. He didn't need to apologise, anyway. She didn't care—they were in the shower—and to show him it didn't matter she opened her palm, taking his dwindling erection against her stomach, using it to spread it all over her abdomen.

He enjoyed her attention until he completely lost all firmness, before pulling a handheld shower nozzle down and hosing her stomach clean. Off in the distance, a phone started to ring.

"Ah, Christ, I've gotta get that," he cursed. "It's probably Mum or Malcolm," he said, seemingly torn. "If I don't answer, everyone begins to worry and they'll show up here en masse to make sure that I'm all right."

"That's okay, go get it."

Llach picked up a towel and stepped out of the shower, towelling his dark hair. Hannah admired his tight ass as he strode out of the bathroom. She lathered her body thoroughly with his spicy scented soap, then rinsed off. She stepped onto the plush bath mat and dried off. She then hung her wet towel along with her damp bra and panties over the towel rod. She wiped the steam from the mirror and looked at her reflection. She needed her blow dryer, but opted for the damp hair tie wrapped around her wrist. Pulling her thick, damp hair into a sloppy ponytail, Hannah left the bathroom in search of her dark obsession.

Hannah didn't have anything dry to put back on. She decided to venture out into the living area to pick up her pants and the blouse that Llach had stripped from her earlier. She'd just slip them on until her underclothes dried.

Still hearing Llach's low voice on the phone, she decided to leave the towel behind and tease him a little. Hannah wasn't embarrassed by her body. She was quite proud of it, actually. And she was pretty sure that he liked it.

Hannah sauntered out and was halfway across the room, which had gone silent, when she realised he was not on the phone and no longer alone. Malcolm was with him. Both men stared at her. Hannah gritted her teeth, unsure what to do. Stop? Run back to the bathroom? The brave thing to do was to continue on and pick up her clothes — they'd already seen it all. What did it matter now?

With a towel slung low on his hips, Llachlan stalked across the room towards her, trying to block his brother's view.

Hannah tried to smile up at him but it came off more like a grimace. He looked angry. "Whoops! I thought you were alone," she began.

"You were wrong!" he growled, scooping her up over his shoulder.

"Hey, Malcolm," she said, smiling weakly, waving awkwardly over Llach's bare shoulder.

Malcolm grinned widely and waved back.

"What the hell do ya think you're doin'?" Llach bellowed as he dropped her on the plush mat inside the bathroom.

"I thought you were still on the phone," she explained, looking up at him.

He scowled down at her, trying to intimidate her.

"I didn't know he was here. I'm sorry. I just wanted my clothes."

"I'll get you somethin' to put on," he barked before leaving her alone.

He stalked back in with a T-shirt and a pair of boxers for her. He stripped off his own towel and climbed into a pair of his own. He gave her another glaring look then turned his back to leave again.

"Hey!" she called to the back of his head. He paused but didn't turn around. She moved in behind him and slid her arms around his waist, pressing her cool breasts to his back.

He inhaled deeply and his hands covered hers, holding her to him.

"I didn't do that on purpose. I thought you were alone. You can't be mad at me."

"Ya just showed my brother all your wares."

She burst out, "My *wares*?" She laughed at the term. It was a word that Lockhart would use. "Oh, he didn't see anything anyway, you were so quick to block me."

"Oh, he bloody well got an eyeful!"

"It could be worse. I could be hideous," she teased.

He snorted and turned in her arms, sliding his around her back. He lifted her so that she was snug against his growing stiffy. "You are hardly hideous. That's why I seem to be in this permanent condition of late."

Hannah stretched and kissed him until he responded. "I'm sorry, Llach. I didn't mean to make you angry."

He sighed and rolled his eyes as he fitted his hands around her backside.

"I'm probably over-reactin'. Apparently, I do a lot of that lately. But I don't want to share ya..." His eyes skittered over the locked heart inked on her chest. It wasn't until that very moment that she realised its significance and what he must think of it. In his mind, it must symbolise Lockhart.

"...With anyone," he finished. "I want ta keep ya holed up here with me. Just you and I. In this castle forever. I don't need anyone else. Just you." His lips closed over hers in a soulful kiss. At that moment, she didn't care who he was. Lockhart. Llachlan. Whoever the hell she was with, she didn't care.

When he released his hold on her, she stared up at him with glazed eyes. What was he saying?

He set her down. "Thanks, by the way." The anger in his voice had faded.

"For what?" she asked dazedly, still very affected from his kiss.

"For this," he said, looking down at the tenting in his boxers.

Her mouth curved provocatively. "I could help you with that," she offered, reaching for him.

He sidestepped her. "You are *so* gonna help me with that. Later. Let me get rid of him. And put some clothes on," he said pointedly before rejoining his brother.

* * * *

"She's the one ya met on the plane? The one ya thought ya knew?" Malcolm's overly interested dark eyes searched Llach's.

"I do know her."

"Aye, inside and out." Malcolm laughed uproariously at the murderous look on his brother's face. "Where do ya know her from?"

"I haven't remembered where yet. But we know each other."

"I don't ever remember meeting her. I think I'd remember meeting that." He grinned, raising his eyebrows lasciviously.

"Fuck off, Malc. She's mine."

"I can *see* that. Doesn't she know where you've met?"

Llachlan hadn't shared any of Hannah's story with Malcolm aside from he'd met her on the plane and thought he might know her. He could already hear the lecture that Malcolm would launch into when he heard it. That was why he hadn't elaborated. Malcolm was so overly protective these days. He wouldn't approve of Llach getting involved with another person going through the same hell that he was. He wouldn't think of it as a healthy decision.

Llachlan knew the minute that Hannah stepped out of the bathroom. He could sense her, felt that she was approaching. It was like an invisible thread that stretched between them. Llachlan observed his brother's face as he turned to watch her. He didn't like it — his brother's unconcealed interest evident. He also sensed that he and Malcolm had enjoyed their sibling rivalry in the past, not that he could clearly recall it, but he felt that in school and in sports that they had tried to outdo each other. But Llach didn't think he could stand to see him flirt or put the moves on Hannah. He might just lose it altogether, on his own brother.

Malcolm's lips parted, making Llachlan look in her direction. She looked like a naughty little nymph just begging to be fucked, and he was up for the job. She had her damp hair pulled into a messy bun giving her the look that she'd just tumbled out of bed after being loved hard. Well, it hadn't been a bed but he'd make damn sure that she woke up in his tomorrow morning, well loved and ready to go again. She had his over-large T-shirt knotted to the side of her hip, showing a little pale swatch of her skin. His boxers were too big on her slim frame and hung low on her hips, giving the illusion that the next step she took might make them fall, unveiling the sweet treat he knew she had inside. And now so did his brother.

Her cheeks sported the prettiest little bloom of colour, a testament to her embarrassment for baring all.

She approached them slowly. She held a hand out to Malcolm. "Nice to see you again, Malcolm," she greeted, looking him straight in the eye.

He chuckled, taking her hand. "It was a great pleasure *seeing* you, lass."

The colour on her cheeks deepened.

"That was a rather shocking introduction to be sure. I must apologise, I thought we were alone." She pulled her hand from his and sat on the stool across from them both around the kitchen counter.

"Where are you from?" Malcolm asked, his eyes narrowing. "I adore your accent."

She snorted. "I'm not the one with the accent," she said cheekily. "And I'm from Canada."

"Huh. Llach didn't tell me." His brows dove.

"Why don't you go on home, Malc? You can see I'm fine," Llach suggested.

"Naw, the pizza's not even here yet."

"You ordered pizza?" Llach asked, surprised.

"Yeah, while you were in there." He pointed towards the bathroom. "Besides, I want to get to know your friend better."

"Mmm, pizza. That sounds great, I'm starving," Hannah said, placing a hand on her stomach.

"You worked yourself up quite an appetite?" Malcolm teased, his eyes twinkling as he tried to embarrass her further.

Her cheeks bloomed again but she didn't back down from the verbal sparring.

"Your brother is quite the taskmaster," she responded.

Malcolm laughed. "Yeah, I'll bet. So what brings you to Scotland?"

Her smile slipped a little. "I was on vacation."

"Were on vacation?"

"She had an accident, Malc. Something she doesn't wish to discuss. Leave off, yeah."

"Oh, I'm sorry, Hannah—Llach—again—didn't tell me." Malcolm's eyes zeroed in on the fading bruise on her cheek and the abrasion on her chin.

"That's okay. My friend and I had this trip planned for years, to see the UK, then she bailed on me at the last minute and I decided to come on my own. I spent a week in England sightseeing, then I went to Wales." Her eyes strayed to Llach's. "I was to spend the next week here in Scotland then the last in Ireland."

"You make it sound as if your plans have changed," Malcolm enquired.

"Well, I hope they have," she said, looking into Llachlan's eyes. His stomach flipped at the implications.

"They've changed, Hannah-lass," he confirmed, taking her hand. "You will not be seein' any wretched leprechauns or Blarney Stones."

She bit her lip to keep from smiling. The look she gave him took his breath.

"You'd better go up to the gates, Malc, or you'll miss the pizza delivery," Llach suggested, not even looking at him.

"Nice segue, Llach. I can tell when I'm not wanted. Crack me open a bottle of red, will ya?" Malcolm said, as he left.

"You'll stay with me?" Llach asked, pulling Hannah from her stool.

"I want to stay," she whispered, climbing into his lap, straddling his hips. She wound her arms around his neck as he tucked his hands under her sweet bottom.

"That's not enough. You make it sound as if sometime you will return to your home. I need to know that you will stay with me." The dread he felt at the thought of her leaving clawed inside his chest.

"At some point I will need to return home. But there is no reason that you could not come with me."

"My home is here, Hannah-lass. Everythin' I love is here." Except for her. He pushed the unbidden thought away for now. "Stay with me."

"Wow, can't leave you two alone for a second," Malcolm said, striding back in with a large pizza box teetering on the palm of his hand. He dropped it onto the counter and helped himself to a bottle of wine from the wine rack. He took out plates as Hannah slid from Llachlan's lap.

"Who wants wine?" he asked, placing three wine glasses on the counter. "Whoops, forgot, no alcohol while you're on the nut-job pills," he said, pointedly to Llach.

Llachlan stiffened at the poorly placed joke.

"None for me, thanks," Hannah said. "It won't mix with my *nut-job* pills, either."

Malcolm turned around and stared at her. Llach knew that she was only trying to help but he also knew what was coming and tried to jump in before the inevitable barrage of questions.

"You seem different today, though," Llach said to her, placing a triangle of pizza onto her plate. She took a dainty bite. "Compared to yesterday," he continued. "You are not so angry or confused. You actually remembered a lot," he conceded, taking a large bite of his own pizza.

"I haven't taken any today. Cassie's the one that insists that I take them. But they just make me feel like I'm drowning, trying to displace vast amounts of water and if I could just break the surface, I'd remember everything." He knew exactly what she was describing. "I did remember a lot. Not that anyone believes me," she said, turning haunted eyes on him.

"I believe you," Llachlan tried to reassure her.

"Only to a point. You don't believe that the things that have happened to me connect to you or your lost time. You said the point is that I believe it but what good is that when no one else will? It's my reality against what everyone else tries to convince me truly happened. And they are so conflicting that I just don't know anymore."

He knew and felt her frustration.

Malcolm sat back down with his glass of wine. His eyes narrowed on them. "Wait, wait a minute, I thought ya met on the plane?"

Llachlan's jaw tightened. They'd said too much in front of Malcolm.

"We did," Llachlan said, stuffing more food into his mouth.

"But you, at least, seem to think that you've met her before, and Hannah thinks that your blackouts are connected to her accident in some way? Do you know where you've met before, Hannah?" Malcolm asked, before dangling the pointed end of the pizza into his mouth and taking a huge bite.

Hannah scored her lip with her teeth. "We met in Wales," she answered, simply.

"*On* the plane," Llachlan was quick to add.

"Is it possible that you met at the hospital? Perhaps you were both just in too much of a drug-induced haze to clearly remember each other?"

"I've only been in this country for two weeks and I definitely spent the first week in London. Cassie showed me pictures that I supposedly sent her. And I was under the impression that Llach's accident happened months prior. There is no way that we were in the hospital at the same time. Besides, I was in Wales and he would have been here in Scotland. Right?"

Both men nodded.

"Do you suffer blackouts too, Hannah?"

"No, not that I know of. I was unconscious for a few days after the…accident. That seems to be where my confusion stems from. I met a version of Llachlan when I was either in Wales or in a coma, depending on which account of my memories you wish to put stock in."

"A version of Llachlan?" Malcolm sat forward in interest.

Llachlan closed his hand over Hannah's. "Let's talk about this later," he warned. The more she said to Malcolm, the worse he would react.

Hannah's gaze shot to Llach's and she picked up on his warning that he didn't want to share all this with Malcolm.

She shrugged. "I guess I was jumped outside the pub and I dreamt of things that don't exist while I was unconscious."

"That kind of sounds like what Llach goes through. He has a whole alternate life goin' on when he blacks out. According to him."

"That's not true. I don't remember what happens when I black out," Llach argued.

"Yeah, ya do," Malcolm argued. "Just not right away. Things return to you slowly and fragmented, but you do sort of remember what you did. Or what you think you did. And then ya just get angry."

Hannah rubbed her forehead as if it were starting to ache.

"You shouldn't stop taking your medication, though, Hannah," Malcolm advised. "It's important, especially so soon after your ordeal. The confusion will dissipate. And in time you will come to realise that what you experienced while you were unconscious was merely your brain trying to entertain you while you were asleep."

She tried to smile. "I'm sure you're right. Excuse me," she said, extricating herself from the awkward situation.

"Christ, Llach, what are ya doin'?" Malcolm hissed in a low whisper. "I mean no offence to the lass—she seems like a great girl from what I've seen, and I saw it all—but ya cannot get involved with her. It's like the blind leadin' the crazy."

"Ya can forget what ya saw right now," Llach said, the warning evident in his deep voice. "And it's too late. We are already involved. I can't explain it. From the moment I laid eyes on her, I can't even begin to describe what I felt...what I feel. It's like I've known her."

Llach heard the bathroom door shut quietly. He knew Hannah thought that he didn't believe her story. It made him feel like shit. But this was exactly why he'd kept it from his family. They just didn't understand what it was like. But in a way he wanted to deny it, too. He wasn't ready to accept that something strange and maybe even incredible was going on. His injured brain just couldn't take it.

"Ya need to go, Malc," he said to his brother.

Malcolm gave him a long look.

Instead of getting mad about it as he'd been doing since he'd woken up, Llach accepted it with the love and concern he could see in his brother's worried gaze.

"I hope ya know what you're doin'," Malc said, pulling on his jacket.

He didn't, but he wasn't about to share that. All he knew was that he needed to be with Hannah.

As soon as Malcolm closed the door, Llach hurried to check on Hannah. He took a deep breath before he knocked softly on the door. "Hannah-lass?"

"Lock?" she whispered.

He detected the different inflection in her voice. She thought it was *him*, calling to her. He fisted his hands and it took every bit of self-control that he possessed not to punch the wood. He couldn't help but feel angry and jealous of this guy that she was looking for inside him. Maybe even using him as a substitute for the man she obviously loved and missed. A man? A ghost? A relative? Perhaps she was as nuts as he felt half the time. He took several deep cleansing breaths as he tried to push the resentment aside. He didn't want to fight.

"Hannah, please, are ya all right? I sent Malcolm home. Please come out and talk ta me," he pleaded through the door. His voice sounded ragged even to him.

"Just give me a sec, Llach, I'll be right out." He could hear in her voice she was crying.

He hovered near the door waiting for it to open. When it did, he took slow inventory of her blotchy cheeks. He smoothed his rough palm over her soft skin. "Please don't be angry with me."

"You made me feel the way that your family makes you feel. Things happened to me. Things I can't explain. And whether you want to acknowledge it or not, what happened to me happened to you too, or we would not know the things that we know about each other."

"I didn't mean to make ya feel that way. I would just prefer not to discuss it in front of Malcolm. They don't understand..."

"Neither do you. You deny it—this...what's going on between us."

"I may deny everythin' else, that I can't explain, but not that. *We* are the only thing that makes sense. To me, it feels right. It feels familiar. It feels like...everythin'," he admitted.

Her eyes softened and she practically melted at his words, encouraging him to continue.

"This, whatever is happenin', is what I've always been lookin' for. I just never knew until now that I was missin' it." He brushed his lips over hers. "You make me crazed," he whispered raggedly. "Everythin' about ya. When I look at ya, when I catch your scent, when ya say my name, your smile. The things that I can see in your eyes that ya haven't even admitted to yourself yet. Things I have not even discovered about ya, all these things call to me. I want to be a part of you." He took her lips in another soul-searing kiss. "Let me be a part of you," he said into her mouth. As much as she tried to blame it all on him, she was just as difficult to reach. In many ways, she was closed off to him. "Let me in," he finished, and slid his tongue deep into her mouth. They might disagree about a great many things but in this one thing, they were in complete sync.

Hannah kissed him back, sliding her arms around his neck. He pulled the elastic band from her hair, then slid his fingers into the dampness, tipping her head back, taking complete control of her mouth. He tucked an arm under her legs and lifted her. He carried her to his bed without breaking contact with her lips.

He gently laid her down, moving beside her, kissing her wildly, his lips and tongue simulating what he had every intention of doing to her. He tossed a leg over hers, straddling her, never breaking rhythm.

Hannah broke the kiss, staring up at him. "Have you been here with anyone else?" she asked breathlessly. It suddenly seemed very important to her to be the only one that he'd brought here. "Have you brought another woman here?"

He relaxed. "No. I have never brought another woman here."

"Are you sure? Maybe you don't remember?"

There was no doubt inside him. "I know it in my heart, Hannah-lass. Trafalis is sacred. This place is ours."

Her eyes filled with unshed tears. She placed her hands on either side of his face and pulled him back to her. She kissed him until he could barely think. Every time she touched him, she drove every thought from his mind save one — fuck.

He wanted to go slow. He wanted to cherish her after the way he'd bullied her out in the stones. It was why he'd been so gentle with her in the shower. But going slow with a woman like Hannah only served to drive her even more wild and impatient, he'd learned. It was a good thing that he had expended at least some of the insane need he had for her or he wouldn't have lasted, but it was difficult when she was so receptive and uninhibited. He wanted to pick her up and impale her, burying himself deep inside her hot, slippery, welcoming pussy.

"Slow down," Llachlan breathed heavily, as she shed her loose-fitting boxers then began to push at his shorts.

"No, I don't want to slow down," she panted, pulling at him. "I want to feel you inside me. *Now!*"

"Now that's an invitation no man could pass up." *Screw it.* He could go slow later. He helped her push his shorts out of the way. She opened her legs eagerly as he settled himself between them.

Llach rubbed the tip of his cock over her ever-ready pussy. "Ahh, you are ready for me, Hannah-lass," he said, arrogantly pleased by how wet she was for him. She dug her heels into the bed and scooted her backside closer to him impatiently. He manoeuvred the head of his erection into her and paused, teasing her.

She slammed her fists against the mattress. "More," she pleaded through gritted teeth. He loved the sound of her desperation.

He nudged into her another scant inch. She moaned and doubled her efforts to force him deeper. "Llach!" she demanded, her legs trembling as she strained to pull him in.

When his name burst from her lips, something inside him flared. He pulled Hannah urgently to the end of the bed, her sweet ass level with the edge, and slammed into her, burying himself in her hot, liquid pussy. He pinned her to the bed with his powerful thrusts.

"Yes!" she rushed, until he pulled up short, remaining still. "Llach!" she whimpered.

He could feel the most amazing leaping little electric pulses bounding across raw nerve-endings inside her tight walls, demanding satisfaction. The exquisite feeling of being sheathed in her tight box almost brought him to his knees.

"Say my name," he commanded, needing to hear her call to him and not her ghostly lover. When she referred to him as Llach, he never knew to whom she spoke. He needed her to be here with him. He slid his arms behind her back until his hands reached her shoulders. He cupped his palms around them, digging his fingers sharply into her shoulders, holding her prisoner, buried to his very root inside her.

Her desire-glazed green eyes met his. "Llachlan," she strained, seeming to know what he needed to hear.

He fought the urge to close his eyes and savour it. "Say it again!"

"Llachlan!" His name was wrung from her lips in a wretched cry.

"Again!" he gritted.

"*Llachlan!*" she screamed.

It was all he needed. He released her shoulders from his grip and withdrew his aching shaft, only to punch into her with long, powerful, satisfying strokes, giving her what she wanted, what they both needed.

She pulled her knees back, giving him full access. He strained in raw, throbbing anguish in an attempt to prolong the silky slide of her smooth pussy. His pulse hammered in his head, his blood rushed through his veins.

She murmured his name over and over in a whispered litany as her inside walls closed in around him, milking him greedily, pulling him deeper into the heaven that was Hannah. He didn't think it was possible but as he lunged mindlessly she became wetter. The thick base of his cock dripped with the proof of her arousal.

He reached, simultaneously stroking a finger around each taut nipple, slowly, until he felt her fiery cunt contract violently as she arched, mewling his name on a strangled cry. He pulled her legs to one side — circling his hips, he ground against her bottom, pumping his hot juice into her. He collapsed next to her, pulling her close. She curled up against him. *We fit together perfectly*, was his last thought before they slept.

Chapter Sixteen

"Hannah..."

Hannah awoke with a start. It took her a moment to remember where she was. *Llachlan.* She smiled slightly when she felt the warm man beside her and remembered all the delicious things they'd done, as he'd promised, all night long. She raised her hand and was about to smooth it up over his chest and maybe wake him for another round when she heard it again.

"Hannah..."

She sat up slowly, looking around the room. The sun was just coming up, filtering light into the darkened room.

"Hannah-lass...save me..."

"Lockhart!" she breathed, getting out of bed. She picked up one of the discarded pairs of boxers and pulled on a shirt, since she had no idea where her own clothes were.

She didn't know where she was going—she just followed the inexplicable pull that she'd felt from Lockhart from the moment that she spied the portrait. She found herself in the room where Llachlan was temporarily storing the portraits until the gallery was completed.

She flipped the light switch and her eyes went immediately to Lock's painting. But she felt the same rush of disappointment as she had the day before when she'd realised that it was not the Lock that she remembered but some other man. An unhappy, ruthless-looking stranger. She approached it slowly just as she had at Jake's.

She looked up, into his eyes. On closer inspection, it did look somewhat like her Lock. His overall features were the same but the tightness in his jaw made him look severe. This Lockhart wasn't alive. There was no life in this man, no inner light in his beautiful dark eyes. She sighed heavily. Just the sight of this Lockhart made her sad. At least in the painting that Hannah knew, the artist had captured his true easy-going, mischievous nature, with that little twinkle, whereas this image depicted a Lockhart that looked as if he had never known joy. He had been disheartened and bitter, tense and angry even before he'd been forced to marry Lillias.

"Save me, Hannah-lass. Save us…"

She started as she heard his voice again. "What are you trying to tell me? I thought you were free?" she asked the flat canvas. "Or was that the other Lockhart and now you need my help too?" She shook her head with incredulity, then laid her forehead on his chest. "I don't understand why you are different. Why Jake was different. Why Trafalis is…changed…"

The thoughts in her head sped up. "That's it. Everything is different!" She moved to pat the painting on the chest but her hand went right through it. "Oh!" She jumped back as she felt the supernatural wind whipping her hair around. "Oh, my God! We fell into it." She remembered the wind and the pressure in her head as they fell.

"Llachlan and I fell into the painting and what we did there as Lockhart and Lillias changed everything! That's why nothing is the same, but like Llach said, even in dreams some things stay the same. We changed Lockhart's future."

"I thought I might find you here." She jumped at Llachlan's voice behind her. The wind stilled. "Do you know how it makes me feel to see you with it?"

"He's not an it and he's you."

He rolled his eyes. "No, he's not me…"

"We changed things," she blurted, not having time to hash this out with him now. She didn't know how long the painting would be open. They had to move quickly.

"What?"

"I've remembered. When I came to you with the portrait and you were showing me around. You were trying to comfort me because I was crying and you took me in your arms and you said, *I feel like I know ya,* and then you moved in like you were going to kiss me and the wind came up and we fell into the painting."

"We fell…into the painting," he repeated slowly.

"I bet it was the same mystical wind that came up and made the board hit you. You said yourself things happen in the Hall all the time that you can't explain. I can't explain it, either, but it happened and we changed things. That's why the portrait is not the same as I remember. And why my Jake is different from the Jake that Cassie and Paul brought to me. Hell, even Paul the dick is different. Come here." She reached for his hand.

He shook his head watching her as if she were mad.

"Come on, we don't have much time."

"And what do you think to do?" he asked hesitantly.

"Go back and put things right."

"Go back? Into the painting?" he said, wide-eyed.

"Yes. Please? You don't understand. I have to make this right for him. I have to make sure that he has a happy existence for one lifetime. Please!"

"And what if we get over there and I don't remember you? Because I don't. I don't remember falling into a portrait with ya."

"But you do, somewhere deep in your subconscious. That's why you say things to me that he has said. I think you are playing his part. Just like I played Lillias. Or perhaps you are his reincarnation. Whatever this is, they need for us to learn our lessons and not make the same mistakes that they did, to change their fate. We are just the vessels they need. But we must have screwed things up for them. Please!" She pleaded with him holding her hand out again. "All that you have to remember is, I'm Hannah and don't you forget it."

As apprehensive as he looked he placed his hand in hers. She positioned her back against the painting but it was solid. "No, no, no!"

"What?"

"It's not open anymore. Kiss me, that worked before."

He shrugged and kissed her.

"You could take the time to enjoy it, Hannah-lass," he said when she didn't respond.

"Sorry. It's not working."

"Perhaps ya could remove your shorts and I could..."

"Stop that. Say the thing," she demanded.

"Say the thing?" he repeated. "What thing?"

"That spell, incantation, whatever you want to call it. That thing that you said before we fell."

"I don't know what you're talkin' about."

"Yes, you do. It's in there, inside you. Think. Let it out. 'Hearts...and hands...'?" she prompted, trying desperately to remember the rhyme.

He looked at her blankly. She made a sound of frustration.

"It was something like, 'home is the heart, hand in hands...keys and...lands'."

His eyes widened slightly. "Heart in home, hand in hand?"

"Yes, that's it!" she exclaimed, taking his hand tightly.

"The keys come from another land," he continued, looking quite stricken that he knew the words. "How in the fuck do I know this?" He stared into her eyes in bewilderment.

"Just finish it!" Hannah encouraged impatiently.

"To free me from this hell on earth, Love's own tear will break the curse."

Just as before, the wind howled and the pressure in her head threatened to explode what brain cells she had left into oblivion. But luckily, the landing was softer this time.

Hannah opened her eyes slowly. She was back in Lockhart's suite. The setting looked the same. There were candles and wine—the same sweet yet pungent scent permeated the room. Hannah looked down at herself and the same pink gown. She tucked her thumbs into the bodice and attempted to pull it up so her boobs wouldn't be on such display to tempt him. She found a discarded shawl and she wound it around her shoulders so that he wouldn't be able to see her skin at all.

She ran over to the wine and hurled it through the tiny arch along with the herbs. She blew out the majority of the candles just as there was a knock at the door.

She took a deep breath before she opened it. When she did, Llachlan or Lockhart stood there, his hand leaning against the doorjamb as if he'd been waiting a long time. He looked down at her as if he were bored.

"You wanted ta see me?" Damn it, he didn't recognise her again. Why was it that she remembered who she was and who he/they were but Llachlan did not remember her? And would it be a bad time to just say his name? No, she discarded that idea. The last time he'd been appalled, thinking she had a thing for his dad.

"No." She tried to close the door on him. If she could keep him out, there would be no chance that they'd have sex. She wasn't sure if she could resist them if she let them in. She didn't feel like she'd just left Llachlan's bed and had marathon sex. She felt horny as hell.

He blocked the door with his booted foot. "You will recall this is my chamber, lass, not yours." He pushed the door open the rest of the way and barged in. He looked around the room then narrowed his eyes on her. "What are ya up to?"

"Nuthin'."

"What is that strange smell?"

"I haven't any idea. It smelt that way when I came in. Perhaps the staff used a new aromatic in cleaning," she made up on the fly.

"I shall have to tell them not to. Now what about you, Lillias, what do you here?"

"I was just leaving. I need to go speak to your father about something rather important. You have a good, um, er, trip to…uh, war and I'll maybe see ya when ya return." She stumbled over her thoughts and yanked open the door wide but he used his weight closing it.

This time she didn't turn around. She remained facing the door, thinking he wouldn't kiss her. She was wrong. He flattened her out against the old wood, his lips finding that sensitive spot just below her ear, sending tingles and goosebumps shooting over her skin. He held her hips as he rocked his hard cock against her lower back.

"Are ya sure ya wish ta leave me now, Lillias? That mumbled bit of nonsense is to be my send off?"

"Aye, I need ta go, your da is waitin' on me. What if he sends someone in search of me and they find us like this?"

He caressed slowly over her ribs, cupping her breasts from behind. Her nipples pearled against his palms and he chuckled in her ear at his ability to arouse her. His fingers met bare flesh where the indecently low bodice ended. Hannah's eyes almost crossed at the overwhelming need he produced in her.

"What have we here?" he asked, with interest in his deep voice. He forcefully turned her to face him. The smirk on his face was diabolical. He knew exactly what effect he was having on her. He unwrapped the shawl from around her shoulders and his eyes warmed by degrees. "Why, Lillias, did you wear this dress for my last night here?" He traced his finger over her bare flesh, following the line of the dress and the curve of her breasts. Hannah trembled at his touch.

"I have to go," she said weakly.

"You don't want to go. I can see it in your eyes. Ya want to stay with me and enjoy my lips on your skin." He lowered his mouth and kissed her hotly. She forgot for a moment that she couldn't allow this to happen. She was about to break away when he did. Pressing his lips down her throat, he pulled down her bodice and went down on his knees in front of her. In her mind, she saw Llachlan kneeling before her in the shower. Wet heat pooled between her legs as she thought of how he'd used his tongue on her. She sighed and threw her head back, working her hands into his hair holding him to her. But he nipped at her too hard, too fast, making her remember what she was doing here. "Lockhart! Stop. We can't do this. You need to leave as planned."

"Ahh, just a little more, Lillias, ya were just lettin' yourself enjoy it."

He seized her nipple crudely. "Stop." She tried to push his head away but he was determined. She'd finally had enough. She fisted her hand around the neck of his shirt and twisted, cutting off his air as she threw her weight forward toppling him over backward. She landed on top of him. But when she got there, he felt really good all hard and wanting. His chest heaved as he looked up at her in surprise.

An evil grin crossed his handsome face. "Ah, so ya like it rough, do ya, lass?" he said, untwisting her hand from his shirt.

She found herself on her back. He threw the heavy skirts up over her face. She struggled, determined not to let this happen again. They couldn't have sex. A child could not result this night or Lockhart would be bitter and unhappy again.

"Wait! Lock. Wait! Let me...let me please you." He stilled. "We cannot do this, but I can satisfy you in other ways."

He pulled the skirts from her face. "And what would you know about that?"

"I don't really. You could teach me. Show me what to do. You can make it so that I know exactly how to give pleasure to you."

He gritted his teeth and moved off her. He offered a hand and helped her to her feet then stood there, unsure, waiting.

Hannah ran her hand down the solid length of him. His chest rumbled. She began to unlace his breeches and ease them from his hips. His cock sprang free. She took him in her hands. His eyes fluttered in ecstasy as if he might pass out at the feeling. She looked down at him. "What do you want me to do?"

He exhaled heavily. "Get on your knees," he said, in a strained voice.

She did and then looked up at him innocently, waiting for further instruction. His chest rose and fell rapidly, his eyes were glazed, his jaw already tight with tension and she knew this was not going to take long. He was already way too excited by the thought of her wanting to give him head, that the actual act would just push him over the edge. Apparently, Lockhart had not been getting much loving in the past.

He shuffled closer, taking her head in his hands. "Take hold. Taste," he rasped.

She took a deep breath, taking his hard cock into her hand, licking the tip softly. She felt a tremor run through him as his hands tightened in her hair. She decided to lay a chaste kiss there as well, as if she were trying to anticipate.

"Use your soft tongue, and lick."

Hannah flicked her tongue quickly over the knob as if she were licking an ice cream cone.

"Slower, not such broad strokes. Tease me. Swirl it. Yesss." His voice deepened on that one word when she took his instruction.

She dithered around the head, pulling down on the extra skin, teasing the sensitive slit. She had to admit—she liked Llachlan's neatly circumcised head better.

"Open your mouth, lass, take just a bit into it. Then a little more." He sounded as if he were in great pain.

She did as he instructed and then, she just stopped.

"More!" he gritted. "Close your lips around...ahh!" he moaned, as Hannah did as he coached. It was difficult for her—she wanted to do what she already knew how to do. And that was please him. She wanted to make him roar with pleasure. She wanted to suck Llachlan's dick. The thought made her cunt heavy and wet.

"Keep your mouth around me and pull up while you suck." She did, making sure to suck a little too hard. Sweet payback for all the times he was too rough with her.

He pulled on her hair. "Ease up, lass, not so hard."

She opened her mouth and released him. He blew out another choppy breath.

"Do it again. But this time take me a little bit farther." She did and he groaned. She felt his hips shift forward, as he tried to feed more into her mouth. She kept his erection in one hand and let her other snake around one side of his toned ass. She gripped it as he clenched and strained, trying to keep hold of himself. She kneaded the flesh as she would ordinarily, trying to encourage him to thrust.

She drew up on his cock with her lips and cheek muscles then sucked gently as he'd asked her to.

"Again," he demanded. She loved him telling her what to do — it was a real turn-on. It was like talking dirty medieval style, without the profane words.

"Let the saliva in your mouth run all over me. Saturate me with your slippery spit. Let it dribble down my shaft. Your lips and hand will slip over me with ease."

He moaned loudly when she did as he asked. She could feel the tension in him thrumming — the juices inside his cock flowing just underneath the thin skin.

"Again, go a little deeper," he panted. She took him farther each time, making her mouth a little firmer, a little more controlled. She wrapped her hand around the thick solid base of his dick and she rotated her hand there, teasing him with the thought that she might pump her fist, along with the mouth action. But she didn't.

He shuffled his feet, widening his stance. She could feel him attempting valiantly to hold back what they both knew was happening.

"Ahh," he rasped. "Go deep. Try and take as much as ya can."

Hannah shifted her knees into a wider stance so that she could move her upper body and really get into it. The tutorial was almost over for both of them and she wanted to give him the full range of her expertise before he exploded. She took him into her mouth as far as she could and made up the rest of the distance with her hand. His ass cheek flexed in her other hand and she accommodated for the thrust of his hips that she knew was inevitable.

"Oh, God, lass, ya learn fast," he said, moving his fingers through her hair.

She released her hand from his tight butt and she curled it around his balls, alternately squeezing and stroking a fingernail over the soft skin underneath.

She gave up trying to feign ignorance. She wanted to please him. She went down on him just as she had yesterday in the shower, and later, too. She knew what he liked and she gave it all to him.

"Ahh... Fuck, Hannah, your mouth is like magic!" he groaned, as he came in her mouth. She savoured every last drop, swallowing.

She stood slowly, pulling his pants up with her. He trembled as he tried to do them up. She would have taken pity and laced them for him but her own aroused brain had only just cleared enough for her to realise what he'd called her in the throes of climax.

"Llachlan?"

He shook his head and looked at her strangely. She knew that the Lockhart inside him would think and probably be grossed out by the fact that she'd just called him by his father's name, but she also suspected that her Llach was right there under the surface. He'd known her...well, at least he'd known her mouth, she reasoned.

She captured his cheeks and stared into his eyes intently. "Llachlan."

He tried to pull away. But she used all her strength. "Llachlan. Fight him—you are stronger now. See me. It's Hannah. Don't you forget! You know it's me. You said my name."

"Hannah?" His eyebrows dove in bafflement. "Hannah?" he said, repeated, his gaze searching hers. She nodded. For a moment his dark eyes glistened and shone from within like the portrait. "Hannah-lass."

"Yes!" She threw her arms around him.

Llachlan held her tight, trembling.

"Are you all right?" she asked, pulling away slightly so that she could look at him. She'd already had time to reconcile this inexplicable event in her mind but he hadn't. She still couldn't quite believe it but it was better than the alternative.

"You were right!" he said, as he covered his mouth with a shaky hand. He sat down slowly on the bed. He huffed an incredulous chuckle. "I can't believe this. Look at ya. Ya look like a different person."

"I do?" she asked, shocked.

"Aye. I believe ya are representin' Lillias MacAllister by the look of ya, and it isn't just the garments. I mean, I can't even explain it—ya look like you to a point but then you just...aren't," he said, confused and unable to articulate it.

Hannah hurried over to the looking glass. She ran her fingers over her face. "I feel doubly lucky now that you finally recognised me. I don't even look like me." She peered closer into the mirror and into her own eyes. "But then again when you look closely, I am here," she said, incredulously.

"Do ya have her memories?"

"Mmm, not really, it's more like just what Lockhart told me. Why? Do you have his? Or do you just retain what memories we have created?"

"I'm not sure. Stepping out of the portrait in Wales and seein' ya for the first time is foggy, I'm not sure if it was me or it is a memory of his. But I almost feel like there was something before that. Maybe I was here alone without ya. When the board hit me in the head." He rubbed the back of his head. "Maybe I've been here many times."

Hannah shook her head at the unreality of it all.

"Do I look like me or like him?" Llachlan asked, seriously.

Hannah walked closer to him. "You look mostly like Llachlan. But you are missing that little dimple that only comes out when you smile."

He couldn't help but do so. He knew what she was trying to do. Her mouth curved and even though it wasn't Hannah's face that he saw, she shone through and lit his world.

"Oh, there it is, I was wrong. You look like Llachlan." She took his cheeks between her palms.

He rested his forehead on hers for a moment, then went to tuck himself back in and lace his trews. He looked down, making a strangled sound. "Would ya like to explain ta me what else is different between the two of us besides the God-damned dimple?" he demanded, staring down at the appendage that definitely did not look like his.

Hannah clamped her teeth together as he jammed the limp, uncircumcised penis back into the breeches and laced them up. He turned on her accusingly.

"That's why ya seemed so surprised in the shower at Trafalis, yeah? How do ya explain this?"

"I can't, honestly. When you came to me in Wales, when you stepped out of the portrait, you came to me in this body. Like Lockhart had to use you in the present time to communicate with me to help release him from the portrait. But he was the stronger one then, the man in charge, but since I brought him home, to Trafalis, you are the one gaining strength."

"So, you *did* have sex with Lockhart, and ya blew him, too. Just now!" he stormed.

"*No!* I just sucked your cock! You just happen to be using *his* body!" she retorted angrily.

"Like fuck! *That* is not my cock! You've been having sex with both of us! This is just too fuckin' weird!" He rubbed his temples.

"You're right, this *is* all too weird. Do you remember being here before, as Lockhart? You were here with Lillias and you had sex with her?" she half-yelled at him. "Do you see me getting pissed off about that? You fucked Lillias, Llachlan!"

His eyes darted side to side.

"You do remember!" she accused. "You took that poor woman's virginity, knocked her up and left her to a miserable marriage."

"But it was him. Not me!" He struggled to put it all together in his own head as well as with Hannah.

She watched him furiously, with her hands on her hips.

"Wait a minute. You said *we* fell into the painting and had sex and made a baby. So, *we* left Lillias and Lockhart to a miserable marriage."

"Yeah, and the pair of you made me endure having my virginity taken twice in one lifetime. That's why women only ever have to suffer that particular misery once. 'Cause it sucks!" she shouted, seemingly becoming more irritated by the minute.

He closed his eyes and shook his head. "So not only do I have his body parts, you had…er, have…hers?"

"It would seem so. At least when I'm here in this time."

All the bluster went out of him.

"I think he is just using you to find his way. I see you when I look at you but there is more, there behind your eyes. Just like you said about me. I'm here but so is Lillias. And we can't be mad at each other because sex was had since it would seem all four of us have been present. A medieval foursome."

He did not appreciate her attempt at humour. "So, now what? How do we get out of here?" he asked, ignoring her joke.

"I'm not sure. I just know that we can't let them make that baby."

"Disappointed?" Llachlan asked, nastily. "You won't get to fuck him one last time?"

"If we ever get out of this, I may never fuck you again. At least he knows how to have some fun and not be such a miserable dick all the time." She shook her head. "You are still having a problem reconciling him inside you. If that's even what this is."

"What do you mean?" he snapped.

"What if it's more like, you know, evolving? When I first met you, Lockhart said that Lillias and he had to learn their lessons before the curse could be broken. Then when you and I were here last, we broke the curse but we changed what their future should have been because we had sex and created their child. What if we *are* them, generations in the future, but we haven't evolved enough to learn and not make the same mistakes?"

"But that would only work if you were a MacAllister."

"Who knows? I could be. My parents were British. And I know next to nothing about my father. It's not too hard to imagine that I might have some Scottish heritage somewhere in my genealogy. Perhaps there was a MacAllister in our past. And that would make sense why Lockhart tried to make contact with me. Maybe he recognised something in me. He used both of us. Or they used both of us." Hannah shook her head—the whole thing was mind-boggling. "What if this is all part of the curse or magic or whatever? What if that crazy witch, in her guilt over Lillias' death, was trying to make amends by casting some other, uh, spell, but she wanted Lockhart to be punished as long as possible first. What if she made us come together like this? But then we so royally fucked things up for them when last we were here that we have inadvertently fucked ourselves over in the process."

"What do you mean?"

"Well, you have to admit, all the things that brought me to Wales were strange. I have always felt this irresistible pull to come here. I thought it was because of my mum. But maybe it was more than that. And what were the chances of me meeting Jake and his gran and finding the portrait in the first place? Not to mention the inexplicable" — she paused to make the quote sign — "'wind' that came up while you were *indoors* working on the castle that caused the board to strike you in the head. And then, the two of us ending up on the same tiny little flight to Glasgow? I mean, really? It's just too far-fetched to be coincidence."

"So, what do we need to do?" he conceded.

"We changed things, and then I went back and I woke up in the hospital. Where were you? You said you vaguely remember stepping out of the portrait. What happened after that? You would have already been in Wales by that time to acquire Lock's portrait. Where did you wake up?"

He turned his back on her. He didn't want to tell her that he had woken up in an alley in Wales not knowing how he got there.

"Hey?" Hannah said, laying a comforting hand on his back. "None of this makes sense, Llachlan. So don't feel like you're going to shock me. Where were you?"

"I woke up in an alley in Wales," he admitted, quietly.

"In an alley?"

"Aye, that's all I know. I don't remember leavin' my hotel room. I don't know what I did. I could have been the one that attacked you. If Lockhart recognised somethin' in you that made him able to escape the portrait, what if I recognised somethin' in you when you returned in this time, and I couldn't control him or me and we hurt you?"

She shook her head. "You didn't hurt me." He still wouldn't look at her. She grabbed his face. "Look at me." She waited until his eyes returned to hers. "Look deep. You did not harm me. You hurt me more by accusing me of things that we've both done." He watched her rein herself in. He knew by the look of steely determination on her face that she would not allow his petty jealousy to cloud her thinking. "Now, let's figure out how to get back."

He looked down, properly contrite. "This is what I hate," Llach raged. "I'm not sure about anythin' anymore. The only thing I'm sure of is we're goin' to end up back in the present, with more lost time on our hands that we won't be able to explain or maybe even remember. And what if we change things again, and not in our favour? What if we go back and make things right for Lockhart and Lillias and they get their happily-ever-after, but I lose you in the process? What if we go back and I never know you? Never meet you? I don't want to take that chance. I don't want to lose you, Hannah." He swallowed hard as the implications sank in. "What if this screws things for us?"

"What are you saying?"

"I'm sayin' that I love ya and I don't want to walk around for the next four hundred years *evolving* looking for ya. I need ya now, in this lifetime."

"I love you, too," she whispered, through her tears.

"Do you? Or do ya love him?" He stared back at her grimly.

"Llachlan!" she shrieked, losing patience. She waved a hand in front of the face that was not hers. "Do you love her?" she challenged, indicating Lillias' features.

"No," he answered, like a petulant child.

"It has always been you. That's why I see you and not him. He may speak through you sometimes — but for me, you have always been you. I love *you*."

He closed his eyes and swallowed her up in a tight embrace. "So what do we do?"

"Lockhart has to, of his own free will, love Lillias, and Lillias, in turn, has to unselfishly set him free," she explained sadly as a tear escaped her eye. "And we have to do the opposite."

He shook his head. "No."

"I have to do this for him, Llachlan. Please. I think that his happiness will directly affect mine. Ours. For our own good, in our own selfish way, we have to be unselfish now and perhaps have the reward later."

"So not only does Lillias have to let Lockhart go, but I have to do the same with you. I have to let you go, unselfishly."

"And I have to love you. And I do, Llachlan. You have unlocked my heart." She softly touched where the tattoo should be if it were her own chest that she was touching. "It has really all come full circle for all four of us. But you and I not only have to love but let go at the same time."

"I don't know if I can, Hannah."

"Have faith. If it's meant to be…it will happen for us. Somehow. Somewhere."

"Some *time*? I don't think I can be as patient as Lockhart."

"But doesn't that just prove to you that if we are meant to be together that somehow we will find a way? Look at them. He's still trying, after all this time. Eventually, all things work out the way that they were supposed to."

He looked down at the floor in desolation and took a deep breath.

"Have faith," she repeated, then she wrapped her hand around his biceps where the Celtic key marked his skin. "And don't you lose the key. You'll need it to unlock me."

"But *you* are the key," he said, looking back at her. "And *his* saviour."

"Perhaps you are the hero in all this, Llachlan."

He made a disparaging sound. Then he nodded, making the decision. He studied her face, his gaze travelling all the way down to her little slippers then slowly back up—finally focusing on her face as if he were trying to memorise everything.

"I love ya, Lillias." His voice shook with raw emotion.

She smiled softly as her eyes filled with tears. "You are free, Lockhart."

The vicious wind whipped around them. Llachlan pulled her tight against him.

Chapter Seventeen

Hannah awoke slowly to a pounding in her head. "Aww," she cringed placing her hand over her forehead. She felt hung over. She was almost afraid to open her eyes. What if she was in a hospital again, or worse?

"Hannah!"

"Cassie?" It was Cassie pounding on the door that had woken her.

"Yes, it's me. I'm coming in whether you're decent or not."

Hannah sat up and pushed at the heavy rich-looking bedspread that covered her. She looked around the room. It was beautifully decorated in rich retro colours, raised wallpaper and brocade trimmings.

Cassie finally burst open the thick oak door. She had a large case in her hand that Hannah recognised as her makeup case.

"I thought you'd be up and hanging out the door," Cassie said, turning to smile at her.

"Oh?" Hannah replied, unsure of what she was talking about.

"Come on, silly. Go get in the shower, so that I can do your hair and makeup." Cassie pulled a giant garment bag off the back of the door and unzipped the most dazzling wedding gown Hannah had ever laid eyes on. Hannah stared at the elaborate, layered, hand-beaded dress and was about to ask who was getting married when she tuned Cassie's voice back in. "There is an impatient Highlander waiting to make you his wife."

"An impatient Highlander?" she squeaked. Could it be? Had they made things right? "Llach?"

Cassie laughed. "Yes, Llach. You can't convince me that you are having cold feet. I've seen you two together. And the way that he looks at you—phew, it's almost embarrassing. He looks like he just wants to drag you by the hair to the nearest cave and have his way with you."

Hannah bit her lip. Could she dare hope?

Cassie turned around and watched her expectantly. "Come on, you don't want to be late, do you?"

Hannah looked at her friend and realised her friend was different. "Oh my God, Cassie, you're pregnant!"

She laughed again, holding her protruding stomach as she did. "How many glasses of champagne did you have last night after Paul and I left, Hannie?"

Hannah bounded out of bed and hugged her friend then rubbed her tummy. "I'm so happy for you."

"Thank you, again. You already said that. It's why I couldn't travel with you for an entire month, silly. But you did all right over here on your own. Snagging and shagging Mr Scottish Hotness, thank you very much. And *I'm* happy for you, if not incredibly sad that you won't be coming home. But we'll alternate vacations every year, okay? You and Llach come to Canada, and then the next year Paul, and this little one and I will come to you. So, let's get you ready."

"Oh, no wait, I have to go see Llach before…"

"No way," Cassie denied, catching her arm. "The two of you — so anxious. I just met him out in the hallway on my way in. He was about to knock on the door. But I stopped him. It's bad luck to see the bride on the wedding day. Jeez! What are guys trying to do tempt fate or something? Go! Shower." She pushed her in the direction of the bathroom.

Hannah marvelled at the beautiful bathroom, all marble and brass, so luxuriously done. She wondered if they were getting married in a hotel.

"Married!" She closed her eyes and pictured Llachlan's handsome face. "Please, God, let us have done this right this time." Hannah undressed and showered.

As she dried off, she looked into the mirror and marvelled at how long her hair was. "Wow!" She looked at herself, trying to see what else might be different. Her body looked the same. Thank goodness. She looked on the inside of each wrist — both maple leaves were still there, the red on the left wrist and the blue on the right. She moved closer to the full-length mirror and looked at her locked heart tattoo. It appeared the same except for the broken chain. It was no longer broken and there was a key attached to the end loop floating happily trailing on her skin. She stared more closely at the key. It was Llachlan's Celtic key. She bit her lip from crying out loud. *Please. Let it be!* Her heart pounded in her chest with excitement and wonder.

Hannah wrapped the towel around her as she left the bathroom.

"Here, put these on." Cassie handed her an ivory bustier with matching panties, including garters.

Hannah stared at her, wide-eyed. Cassie raised her eyebrows. "You picked them out. You said he'd have fun removing them...with his teeth."

Hannah smiled going back into the bathroom. She contorted her way into the bustier and put on the panties and garters. They did look sexy, she thought, turning to look at all sides in the mirror.

"Wow!" Cassie commented as Hannah returned. "If he knows what's under that dress, you will be leaving the reception early. His brother already has a pool going on that front. I wagered twenty pounds on an hour into the reception before Llach carts you off."

Hannah laughed sitting in front of the round mirror.

"So, what did you decide? Do you want to go with the curly up-do that we tried out with the veil, or do you want to wear your hair down."

"You decide, Cassie, what do you think?" Hannah had no idea what the veil even looked like. "Did you like the up-do best?"

"Yeah, you know I did. You wear your hair down every day — you want to stand out today. Not like you won't with that amazing hunk of man beside you. But everyone is going to be looking at you today."

"'Kay. Do your thing, then. Make me beautiful for my amazing hunk of Highlander."

"I don't need to make you beautiful. You already are. And since you've been with him you absolutely glow."

Hannah took a deep breath.

"Hey, what's that?" Cassie asked. They both looked at the piece of paper that slipped under the door.

Cassie toddled over and bent over stiffly to pick it up.

"'To my beautiful bride', it says."

Hannah wiggled her fingers for the paper and only then realised the big rock on her finger. "Whoa!" she breathed, looking more closely. Her engagement ring was stunning.

"Oh, will you quit admiring that Celtic knot already, as if we mere mortals aren't envious enough. What does the note say?"

My dearest Hannah-lass,

I woke up this morning in a strange bed with a pounding headache when my brother burst into my room and informed me that I was getting married today.

It would seem that I have lost time again and I hope that my lost time matches yours. And I pray that if we changed things, that we have not changed. And I hope we get to remember all the great stuff that happened between us that led us to this day.

I feel happy. I feel alive. I feel excited about the future. I have not felt like this…maybe I have never felt like this. I can't wait to see you, Hannah, and make up for all our lost time.

I love you, for all time, my Hannah-lass. Heart in home, hand in hand.

Love, Llachart

"Llachart?" Hannah whispered in awe, wiping a tear away.

"Yes, Llachart," Cassie chided. "Who did you think it would be from, silly?"

Hannah folded the letter quickly. She hadn't realised Cass was reading over her shoulder.

"What's his middle name?" Cassie asked, looking off into the distance with a dreamy stare. "With such a romantic first name, I can just imagine."

"I'm not sure," Hannah shrugged.

"Well, you two *are* getting married rather quickly. I guess you don't know everything about each other. But you'll have time right?"

"Yes, time. Lots and lots of time," Hannah repeated.

"What does he mean, if you changed things? And lost time?" Cass asked, brushing out Hannah's long dark hair.

"He just means, you know, we were both floating around through life going nowhere until we met. We were lost, ya know. And then we found each other. And by changing, he just meant that even though we are getting married and things will change, we won't change. We'll still be, you know, us." She shrugged, hoping that bit of nonsense sounded plausible.

"Oh my God, Hannie, did you luck out with this guy or what? He's gorgeous *and* romantic!" Cassie sighed and started pinning her hair.

"Yep, I hit the jackpot."

* * * *

"Llachart! Stand still, for Christ's sake. Ya are drivin' me to drink," Malcolm scolded, pulling at Llach's tie. "You'd think by the way you were actin' that you were anxious or somethin'," he teased his younger brother.

"I am. Go hurry up Da. I'm set. Go get everyone else ready," Llach retorted, slapping his brother's hands away. "I want to walk my wife up the aisle already."

"Well, I suppose I would be anxious to walk her up the aisle, too. Ya lucked out this time, Llach. Hannah is not only stunnin', but she's smart and witty and fun to be with and…"

Llach smiled at his brother as he fished for the right word for his bride.

"Timeless…Hannah is timeless," Llachart finished.

"Aye, and that right there is why the ladies fall at your feet."

"I don't care about any of that. There is only one woman, and I want her by my side."

"Well, let's get you married then, yeah?" Malcolm agreed, grinning.

* * * *

Hannah stood at the top of the staircase that led down into the portrait gallery of Trafalis Hall. They were not in a hotel at all. She looked around in awe and pride. The hall was amazingly beautiful, not only decorated for the wedding, but the castle itself was once again intact and majestic.

"Oh, that Munro plaid is beautiful," Cassie admired, shaking out the train on Hannah's dress one more time. "The crimson stands out so strikingly against the white." Cassie stood up, panting at the over-exertion.

"Hey, enough, you've done everything you need to do," Hannah said. "Now go be my matron-of-honour and I'll see you down there."

"Okay," she said, straightening her own dress. She handed Hannah a bouquet of red roses and ivy with a ribbon of Munro plaid tied around it in long curly trails so that it would show up against her dress as she walked down the aisle.

She felt like a princess.

"Oh, here comes Llach's dad. I love you, Hannie. Be happy," Cassie said, turning then to the gentleman approaching the landing. "She's all yours, Mr Munro."

"Och, for as long as it takes ta walk her down the aisle and then she's my son's. Are ya sure ya want ta be saddlin' yourself with the likes of him for all eternity?" he teased, smiling affectionately. He was a handsome man. Hannah could see Llach in him. His father's name was Kerr, she remembered.

"I want nothing more than to be saddled with him for all eternity." Hannah smiled.

Cassie chuckled and held the rail as she waddled down the stairs. "I love you, too, Cassidy," Hannah called after her. She turned and smiled.

The music started.

"Are ya ready, Hannah?" Kerr asked.

"I'm so ready."

"So is my son." Kerr pulled the veil over her face. "You look lovely, lass."

"Thank you." She beamed. She was so pleased with everything. The dress, the Hall—everything was perfect. Cass had done a wonderful job on her hair, leaving little wisps, giving her a soft look along with the veil.

They walked slowly down the stairs, arm in arm. Hannah wanted to run but with the high heels and the massive skirt and train, she had no choice but to hold onto Mr Munro tightly. And she didn't want to make a fool of herself in front of her new family. She felt a lump in her throat. A family. It had been a long time since she'd had a family. She missed her mum today. She hoped she was watching.

"Oh, there are a lot of people!" Hannah exclaimed, when the guests stood as she and her future father-in-law approached.

"Aye, we're a big family, lass."

They all stared at her but she looked ahead, eager to see the face that she needed to see.

As soon as he came into view, it was as if time stood still. Hannah's eyes met his and a thrill went through her. "Llachlan," she whispered.

His face softened and he smiled slightly as his eyes explored hers, searching for any changes through the veil.

Llach couldn't wait for his father to bring Hannah to him. He was moving entirely too slow. Llach started towards them. She dropped his father's arm and the bouquet and hurried to meet him. She stopped as she reached him. He lifted the veil, tossing it over her head, devouring her beautiful face with his eyes. His hands came up, circling her lovely face.

"I love you, Lockhart," she whispered, looking up at him with shiny eyes.

He grinned, trying to ease her worried gaze. "You are free, Lillias."

"Ohh," she breathed, throwing her arms around his neck. He kissed her soundly, forgetting all about the guests until his father and brother started patting his shoulder rather urgently.

Llach reluctantly released her lips. He grinned cockily at the way she stared up at him dazedly. "You'd better not let my wife see ya lookin' at me like that, lass."

"You're not married yet, ya dolt," his brother said, taking him by the arm and dragging him back to their places in front of the minister.

Cassie rushed to Hannah and pulled her veil back in place and straightened the train, handing her the bouquet. "Thanks, Cass."

"You sure know how to make an entrance, Han." Cassie smiled, indulgently.

"Sorry, folks," Llach addressed the crowd. "They've kept her away from me for almost twelve hours—you'll have ta forgive me." A murmur of laughter moved through the guests and a blush of colour bloomed on Hannah's cheeks, only partially hidden behind the veil.

Kerr took her arm and they walked the rest of the way to Llach. Hannah passed the bouquet to Cassidy. Llach's father placed Hannah's hands in his son's and gave her a quick peck on the cheek. "Be happy," he said to them both.

The minister began the ceremony with a blessing, ending with, "And ya see why they must be wed, aye?"

Hannah bit her lip from smiling and looked up at Llachlan.

The minister continued, "If there is anyone who would contest this union, speak now…aww, who are we kiddin'?" The guests chuckled again. "We'll just get on with it, will we?"

"It would be nice, Reverend, I feel like I've been waitin' four hundred years for this!" Llach quipped.

The ceremony went by in a blur of tears. Llach even shed a few when he recited his vows, especially when Hannah gave her teary, heartfelt promises to him, even though she stumbled over his name and called him Llachlan. But she didn't even need to repeat the words at all—he could see everything she was feeling shining in her expressive green eyes.

"I now pronounce ya husband and wife. Ya may *now* kiss your bride, Llachart Munro," the minister announced.

"Gladly, Reverend, I thought you'd never ask." Llach lifted her veil. "It's about time."

"Ya never were long on patience, lad," the cleric chortled.

Llach chuckled as his lips touched Hannah's. He kissed her until his brother tapped him on the shoulder. "Llachart, any time now. Some of us would like a wee dram."

Llach released Hannah's lips. His eyes were lit from within, just like they'd been in the original portrait of Lockhart. He seemed so happy and relaxed. She didn't know this side of him. He'd always been so serious, but then again, their circumstance had been severe.

He offered his arm with a flourish. "Shall we, Mrs Munro?"

"It would be my pleasure, Mr Munro."

They walked down the aisle and were immediately swarmed by people with well-wishes and photographs, barely giving them a moment to themselves.

"That's enough, everyone. I'd like to dance with my bride before our first anniversary," Llach joked. "Let's go dance and eat and get my brother tanked."

"Wait, Llach," Kerr broke in. "We need to take one last photo for the wedding portrait."

"Of course." Hannah looked to him as the photographer aimed. "Wait," she said, looking around at the portraits that were behind them.

"What is it?" Llach asked with concern.

"I want the photo taken with Lillias and Lockhart's wedding portrait in the background, so that when the portrait is painted, the artist can incorporate it into ours." Llach's eyes softened. "We owe them…everything," she added.

"It's perfect," he agreed.

He led her down the west wing. Hannah looked up at Lockhart's painting and bit her lip trying to control her tears. He looked like Llach again. He stared down at her, smiling, his eyes glinting with devilment. "Did he get his happy ending?" she asked, looking to Llachlan.

"I'm not sure, Hannah-lass, I don't know what else we've changed. My mind is still hazy. Let's have a look."

They moved to the next portrait. "They look happy," Hannah said.

"Don't you remember the story of Lockhart and Lillias, Llach?" Kerr asked.

"Mmm, no, I'm sorry, Da, I don't."

"If you two are going to run this place so that your mum and I can run off and see the world, you'll need to know these things." Llach and Hannah exchanged a look. "But I'll forgive ya because of the wee bump on your head, yeah," Kerr teased his son affectionately. "It is said in the genealogy that young Lockhart and Lillias had quite the energetic, uh, sex life." Hannah and Llach exchanged a look of amusement. Apparently they'd corrected many things for Lockhart and Lillias.

Llach bent to whisper in Hannah's ear. "That's because Lockhart enjoyed your hot, sweet, talented mouth, thinkin' it was Lillias. And perhaps she kept your memories as you kept hers. Then she was well prepared to please him and herself as well." He grinned mischievously.

Hannah blushed as Kerr continued, "It was well documented that they were caught many times by the household staff in different, uh, rather compromising positions, shall we say, in all parts of Trafalis Hall and the grounds as well. And the brood of children they bore together would back up these accounts. Nine, I believe, in all."

"*Nine!*" Hannah exclaimed, her smile slipping, while Llach's grin grew wider as if his prowess had something to do with it. His dark brow shot up.

"Don't even think about it, buster!" Hannah shot at him.

"Again with the buster," he laughed.

"Can we get drunk now?" Malcolm complained, leaning next to one of the portraits.

Hannah and Llach posed in front of the portrait of Lillias and Lockhart then were dragged into a luncheon and reception. They sat down at their table and were finally given a moment to talk alone.

Llach smoothed a finger down the side of her cheek. "Can ya believe this?"

"I told you to have faith." She smiled lovingly into her new husband's eyes.

"Aye, that ya did." His gaze grew serious. "Has anything changed for ya?"

"My tattoo has."

He looked down at her wrists. "The Lockhart one?" he asked.

She nodded.

"How?"

"My lock has found its key and it looks suspiciously like this one." She wrapped her hand around his inked biceps.

"That's interesting. My key now has the words *Have Faith* written under it in lovely flowing script."

She smiled. "I can't wait to undress you and see it."

"I was thinkin' the same thing about you, Hannah-lass."

"I wonder what else has changed?" she said, looking out at the sea of people watching them, her eyes landing on the biggest change she'd seen so far,

Cassie's rounded tummy. "Trafalis is beautiful, Llachlan...er, Llachart." She giggled.

"I know, the auld Hall is more than I'd ever imagined," he said proudly. "Ya know, I don't even remember bein' called Llachlan. To me, I have always been Llachart in my mind. But it doesn't matter what else has changed. We broke the curse and freed Lockhart, we made it so that he and Lillias could enjoy each other and their time together, and we found each other. This is our time. I couldn't ask for anything more. I love ya, Hannah-lass."

He kissed her again, overwhelming her with need.

"Will ya get a room?" Malcolm said, placing two flutes of champagne in front of them.

"I lied," Llach said.

She looked at him, confused.

"I could ask for somethin' else. For all these people to disappear so that I can take my wife up to our suite so I can make love to her."

She smiled, placing her hand on his thigh under the table and squeezing. He gritted his teeth and growled deep down in his chest.

Malcolm tapped a spoon on his glass to call everyone's attention.

"Everyone, I'd like to make a toast to my brother and his beautiful new bride. It was hard enough to be Llachart Munro's older, less good-looking brother *before* he married the most beautiful girl in the world. Now I am poor Llachart Munro's *older*, *unmarried* brother, who will now be openly pitied and or pelted with rotten vegetables." The guests laughed. "But seriously, folks, how can I compete with the story that brought these two beautiful people together? The beautiful Hannah Keys travels all the way from

Canada to Wales only to be set upon by ruffians, then saved by none other than my brother."

Hannah and Llach exchanged another look of surprise. "My hero," she said, moving her hand ever higher on his thigh.

Malcolm continued, "As if he wasn't born with all the looks and all the smarts, he gets the girl and also achieves super-hero status. I hate overachievers." The crowd laughed. "But I love my brother, cape and all," Malcolm said, turning to toast Llach. The brothers exchanged an amused if not affectionate look. "So, a toast." Malcolm raised his glass. "To my brother, Llachart, and my new sister, Hannah. May they spend the rest of their lives feeling the way they do at this very moment."

Glasses were raised as the guests toasted the newly married couple.

"Oh, and one more thing," Malcolm added. "The first person that taps the glass to denote a kiss from the happy couple will be thrown outta here because if he starts kissin' her now, he'll never come up for air," he said to the chortling crowd then he turned to Hannah and Llach and said in a lower voice, "I have a feelin' you two are gonna make Lillias and Lockhart's antics look tame."

Llach roared with mirth. "I'm up to the task."

Malcolm rolled his eyes. "When aren't ya?" he laughed, walking away.

"You're different," Hannah said, turning to look fully at Llach.

His face lost some of its shine as his dark eyes searched hers, his brow puckered. "Ya think so?"

"You seem so happy and carefree."

He looked relieved. "Is that a problem?"

"Not at all," she answered, shaking her head as she continued to stare at him.

"You are lookin' at me that way again." He grinned. "Do ya think I am gorgeous?" he teased.

"I think you are gorgeous and hot and all male aggression with exquisite technique," she said, moulding her hand over the bulge in his kilt. "And I can't wait for you to use your skills and make me your wife," she invited, smoothing her tongue over her bottom lip.

He exhaled heavily. "And you, my Hannah-lass, have not changed at all, thank the good Lord. Ya can still drive me to act the caveman."

He ensnared her wrist and pulled her up and over his shoulder in one big swoop, fireman style. She shrieked as he beelined for the stairs.

"Wup! There they go!" Malcolm roared. "I win the bet! Drinks are on me!"

The guests cheered.

Llachart sprinted up the stairs as if she weighed next to nothing, booted the door to his suite open and tossed his new wife on the bed. His eyes were burning hot and determined.

He pulled up the layers of her skirt and dove in. Hannah giggled until she felt his hot mouth nipping at her panties. "No, wait!" she said, sitting up and pushing her skirts down. Llachart stilled.

"Stand up," Hannah commanded of him. "Let me see!"

"See what, Hannah-lass?" He stood, perplexed.

"Lift up that kilt."

He grinned. "Ahh, I see, ya wish ta know if a real Scotsman doesna wear anythin' under his kilt?"

"Oh! Yeah, well, I guess that, too."

He cocked his head to the side, confused, as she lifted the tartan. She smiled happily and if he weren't mistaken, he saw relief on her face.

"Now what's that about?"

"I'm just happy to see...you." She smiled, biting her lip. She circled her fingertips around the smooth tip of his perfect cock.

He threw his head back and barked with laughter. "So I did have an advantage over auld Lockhart after all, it would seem."

"Aye," she said, playfully. "Let's just say I prefer more modern customs."

"Me too." He wiggled his eyebrows as he tried to get under her skirts again.

"No, wait." She stopped him.

He gritted his teeth. "You were far more agreeable when you didn't even know our name," he said, thinking back to how easily she'd come to him in the kitchen at Jake's.

She stood and turned her back on him. "Unzip me. You'll like it."

He did as she asked, unzipping the lovely gown. She slid the arms down and let the gown slip to the floor, careful of the veil still fastened into her hair. He watched her long beautiful legs as she stepped out of the enormous skirts, strappy, sexy high heels on her feet. *Garters.* His breath accelerated. His gaze travelled over her sweet ass, and she turned, showing off the ivory, corset-laced bustier pushing her lovely breasts up nicely. He would remember her this way even when they were old and grey.

He growled deep in his chest. "Ya should have walked down the aisle just like that, Hannah-lass." His lip curled in that Neanderthal, predatory way of his.

"Then you never would have made your vows," she said, backing towards the bed, anticipating the pounce that was to come as he stalked her. "And I never got my first dance." She pouted prettily.

"Oh, we're gonna *dance*, Hannah-lass, it's just gonna take us all night long," he promised huskily right before he took her down. "Or better yet, love, we'll spend the next seventy-five years or so this way."

"Seventy-five years? That sounds ambitious. I'll be nearly a hundred," Hannah said, curling into him and kissing the hammering pulse at the base of his neck.

"Och, you're just a babe compared to some, eh?" He grinned cockily.

Hannah's laugh died on her tongue as he took it into his mouth. She was deliriously happy. She'd just married the man of her dreams. A modern-day Llachlan and seventeenth-century Lockhart all rolled up into one beautiful, strapping Highlander. She had the best of both men combined in Llachart. Hannah kissed him feverishly, determined to spend the rest of this lifetime making up for lost time.

About the Author

H-K lives in Canada with her hard-working hubby. She has two very handsome grown sons and a beautiful teenage daughter.

She has been an avid reader all her life. Her first love is historical romance so it would come as no surprise that her favourite book of all time is Jane Eyre. But she'll read almost anything that captures her attention and imagination. She loves nothing more than to find a good book that she can't put down. She is a hopeless romantic and prefers happy endings.

HK Carlton loves to hear from readers. You can find her contact information, website details and author profile page at http://www.total-e-bound.com.

Total-E-Bound Publishing

www.total-e-bound.com

Take a look at our exciting range of literagasmic™
erotic romance titles and discover pure quality
at Total-E-Bound.

www.ingramcontent.com/pod-product-compliance
Lightning Source LLC
Chambersburg PA
CBHW030139180626
46812CB00002B/753